POKÉMON™

PIKACHU MEETS EEVEE

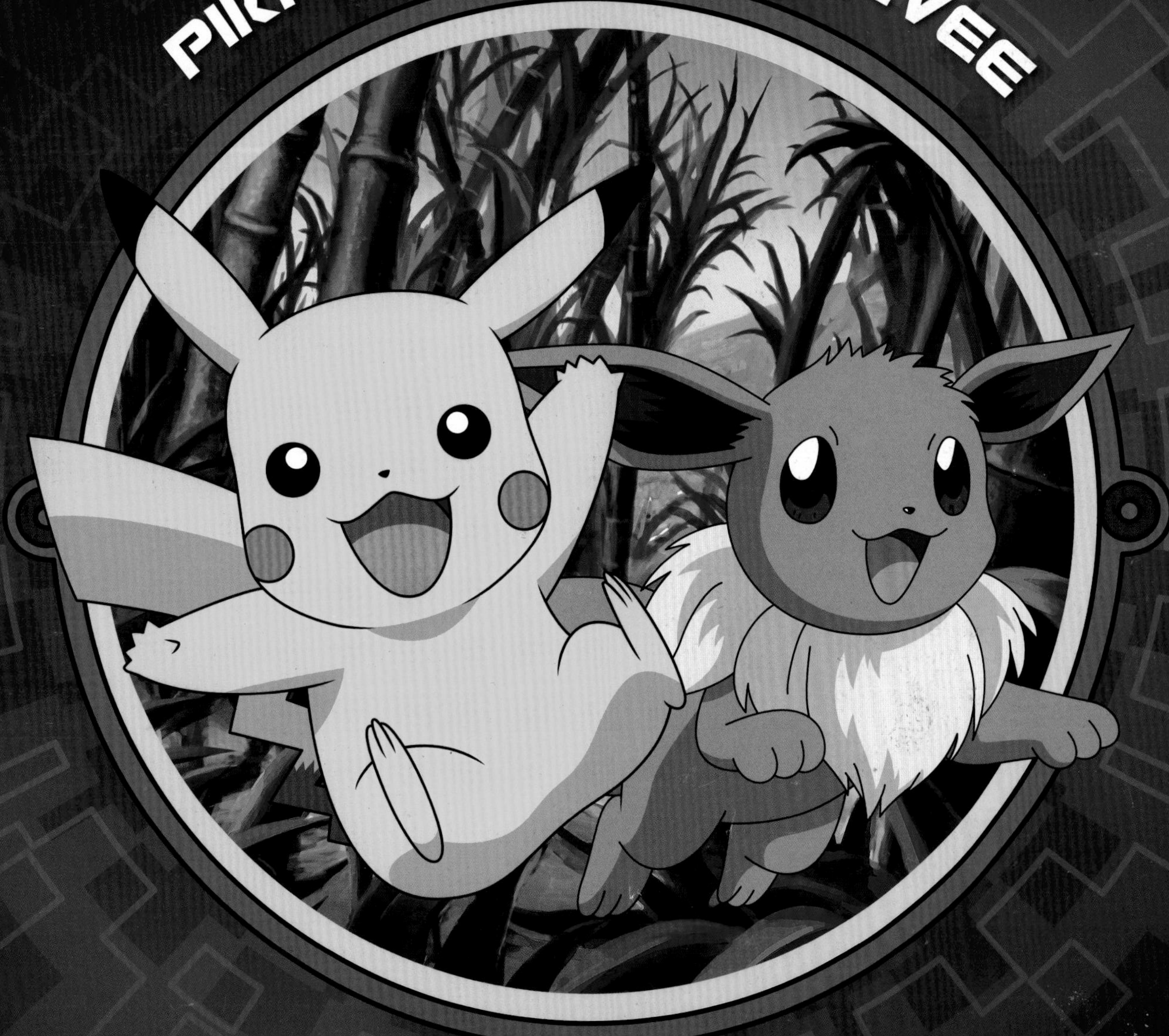

VIZ media

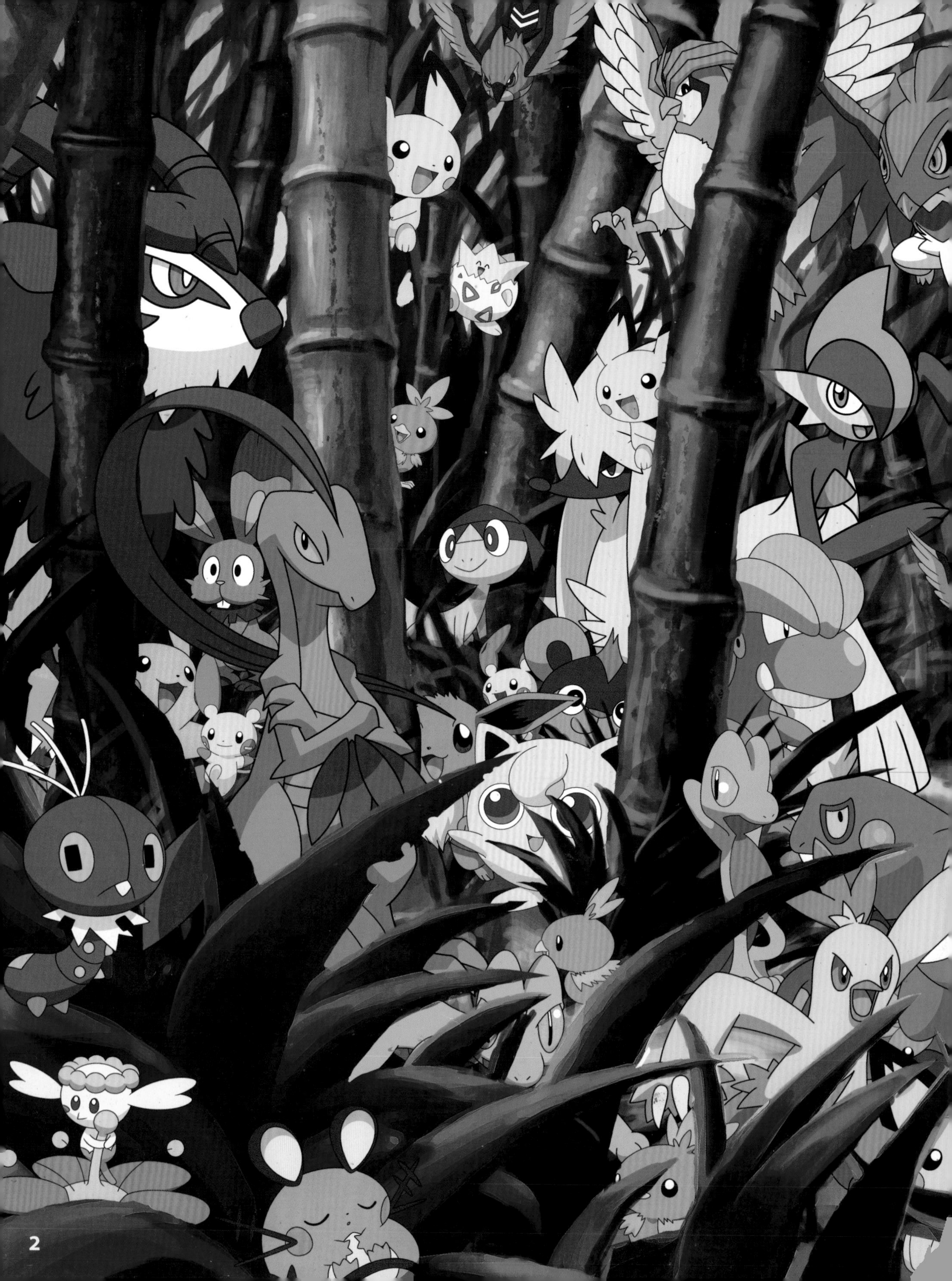

IN THE FOREST

Pikachu and Eevee are taking a walk today. Eevee wants to show Pikachu all its Evolutions. In the bamboo forest, they meet Leafeon, the Grass-type Pokémon, and they all play hide-and-seek. Can you find Pikachu and Eevee?

LOOK FOR...

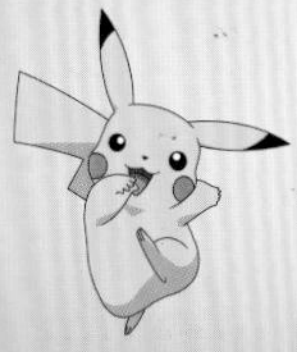

Pikachu

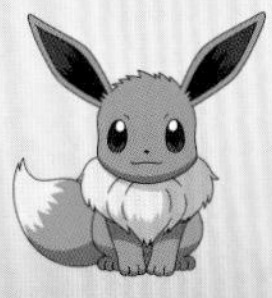

Eevee

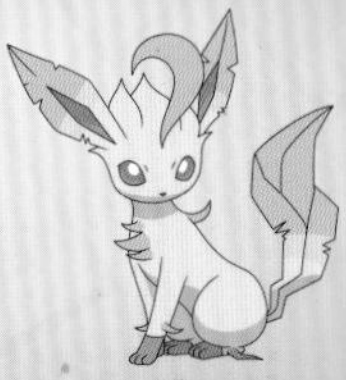

Leafeon

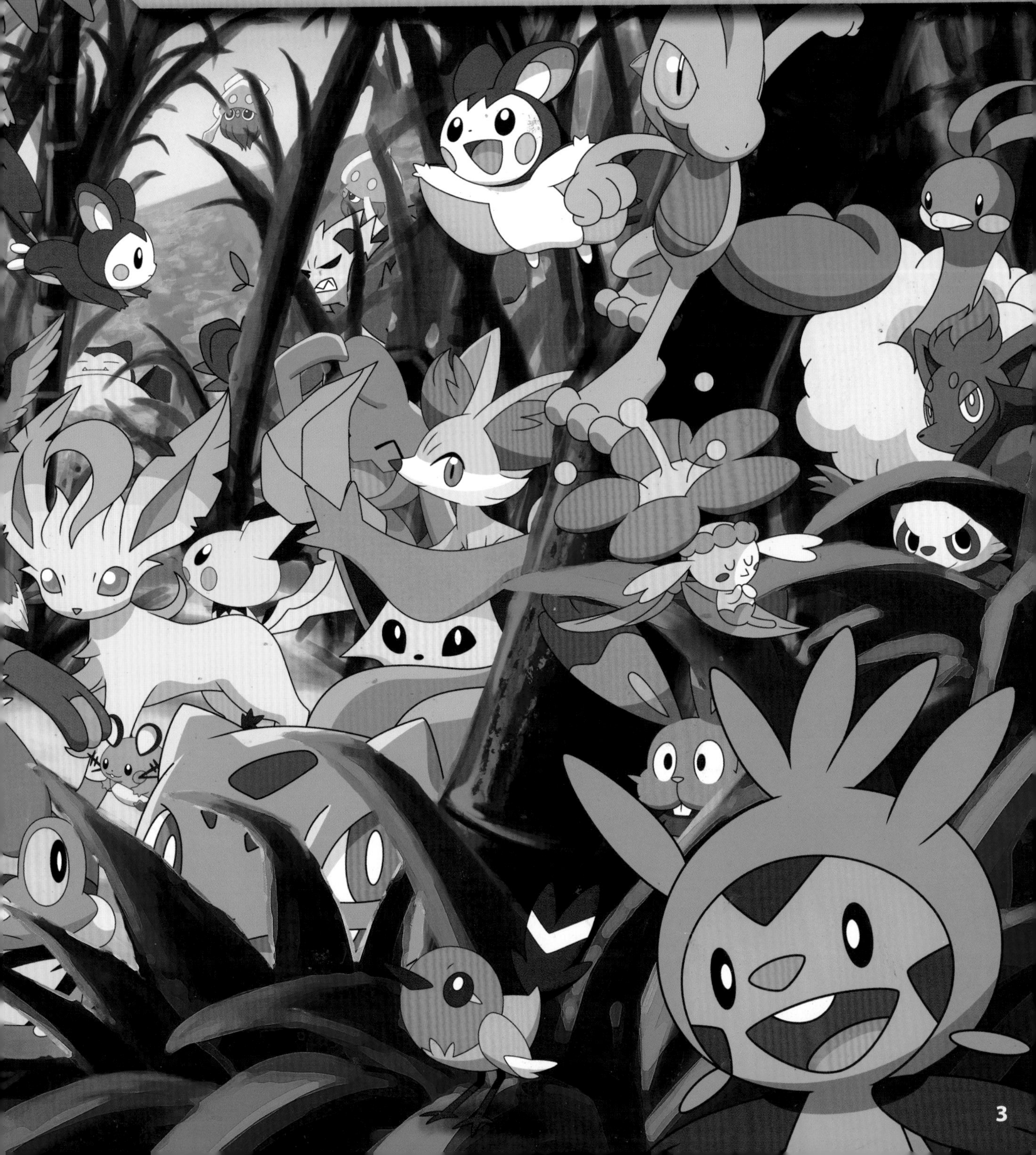

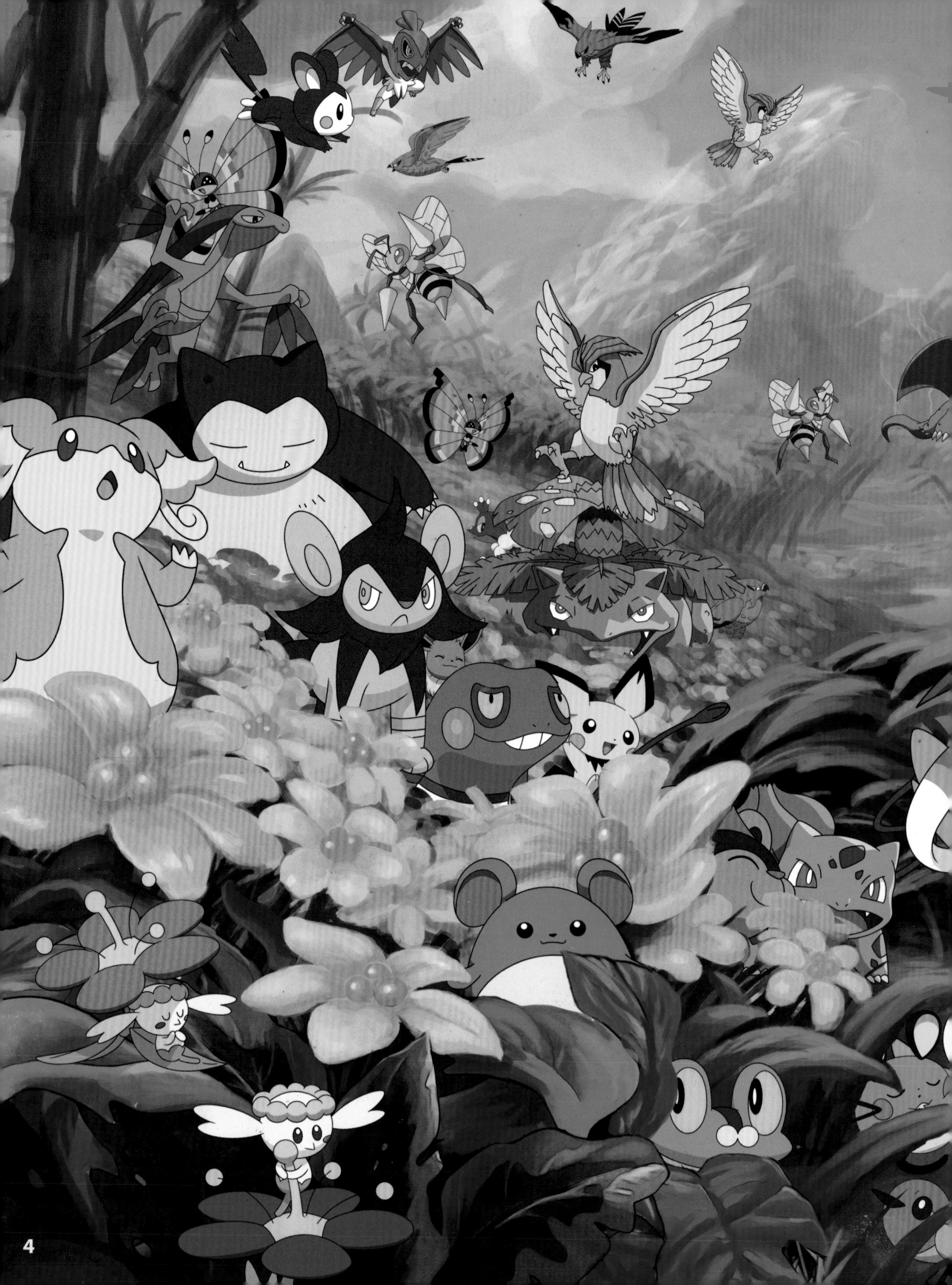

WELCOME TO PARADISE!

Our two friends find themselves in the countryside where the charming Pokémon Sylveon lives. Pikachu and Eevee follow Sylveon through the flowers. Let's find them!

LOOK FOR...

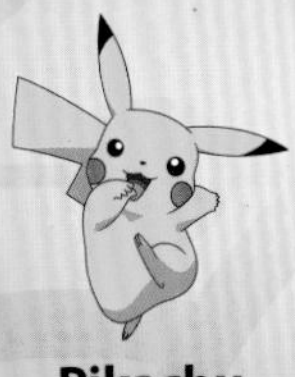

Pikachu

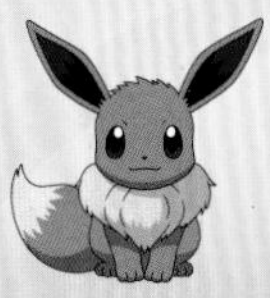

Eevee

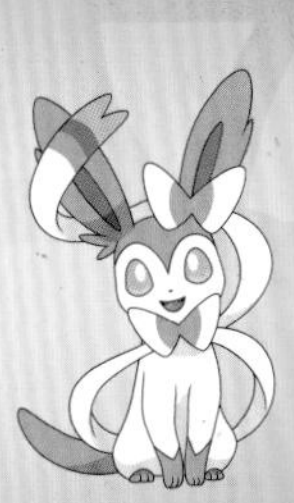

Sylveon

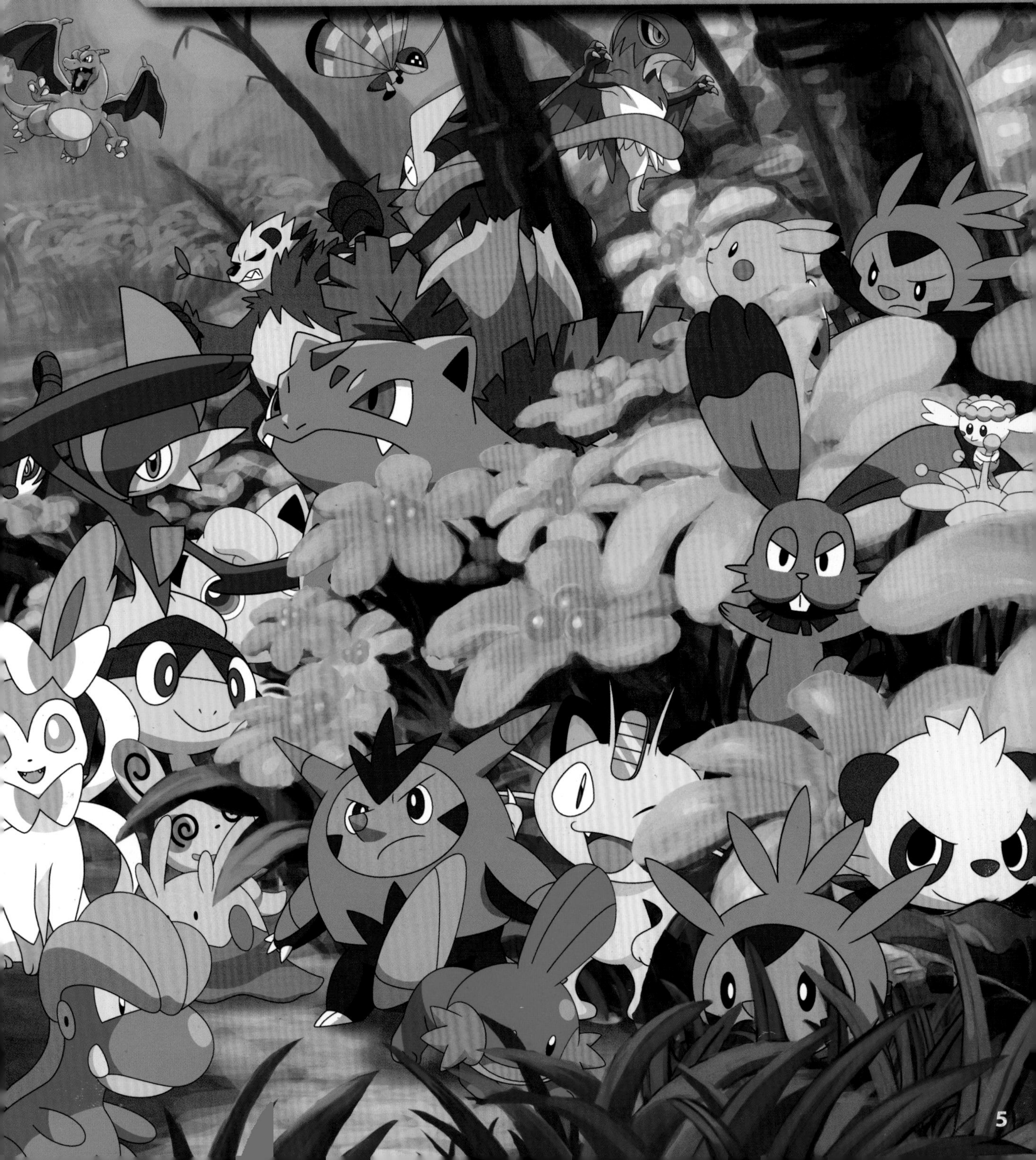

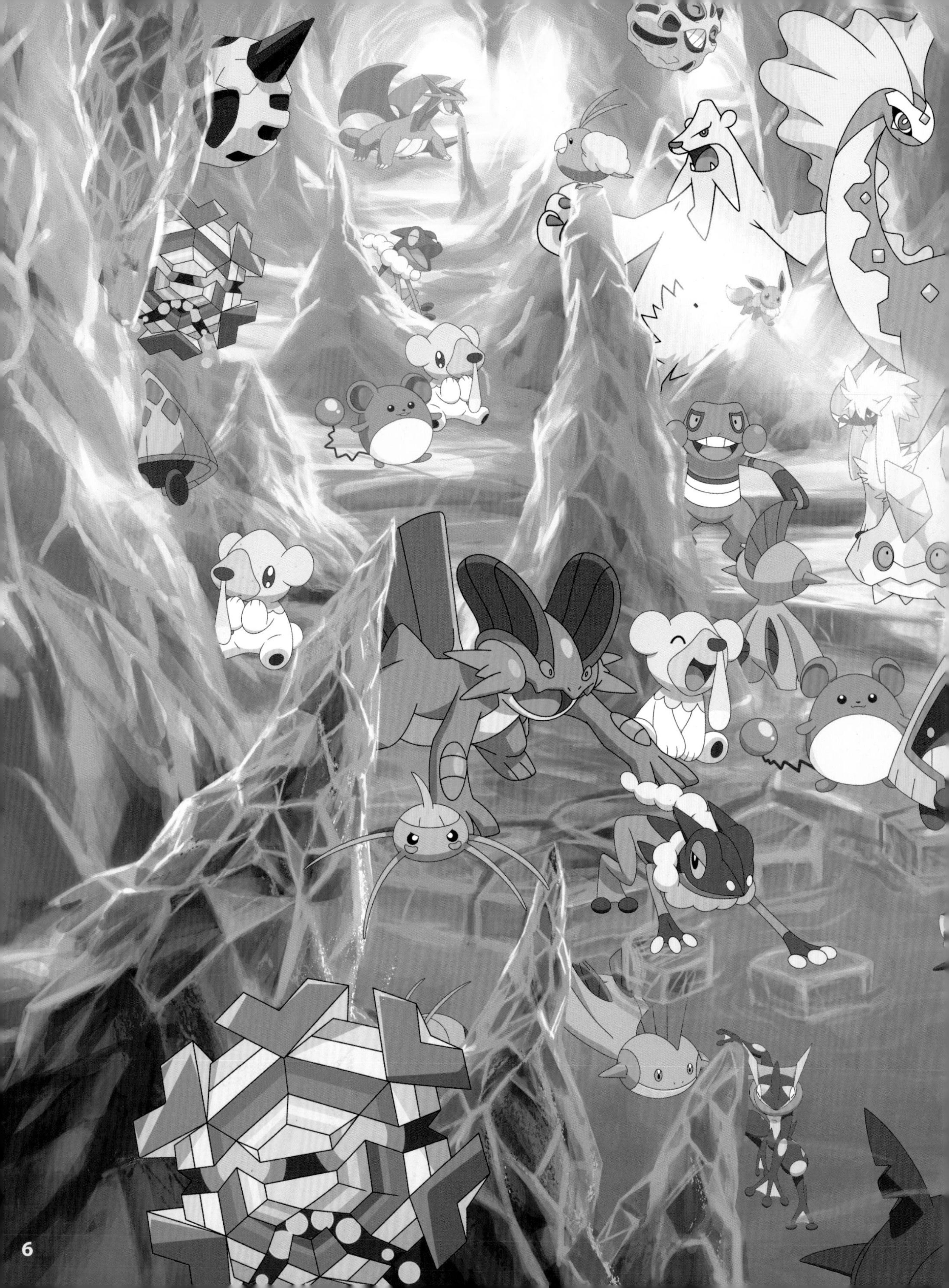

A WORLD OF ICE

Our friends find a path that leads to Glaceon's ice palace! Glaceon sleeps peacefully while all the other Pokémon have fun. But where have Eevee and Pikachu hidden themselves this time?

LOOK FOR...

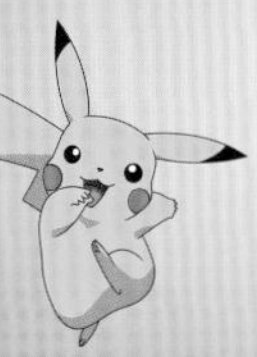
Pikachu

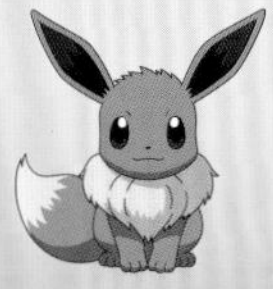
Eevee

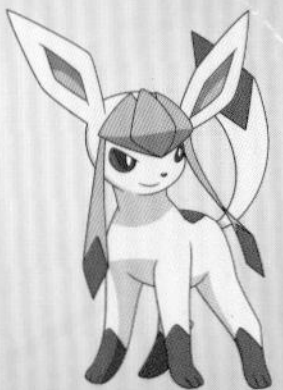
Glaceon

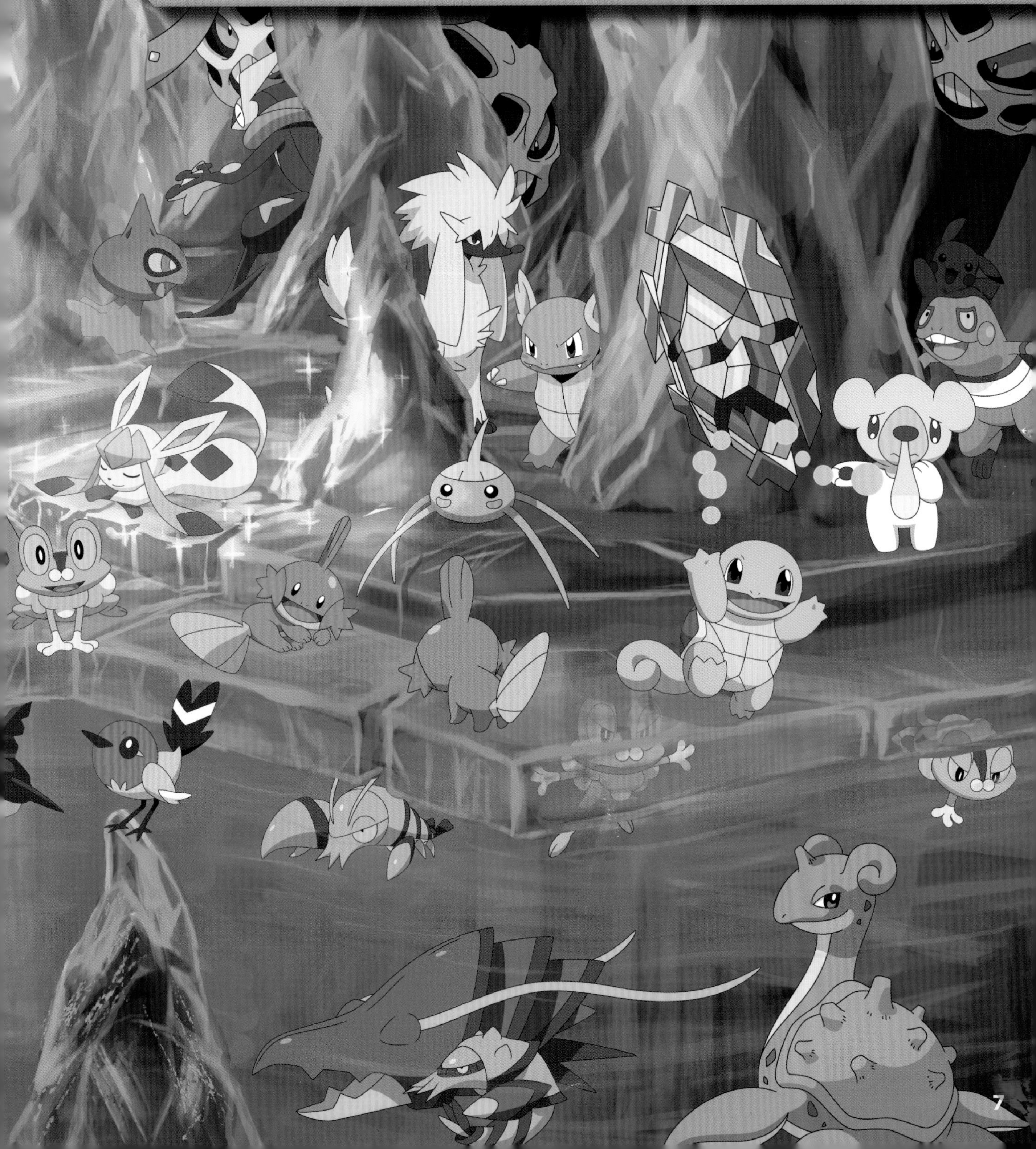

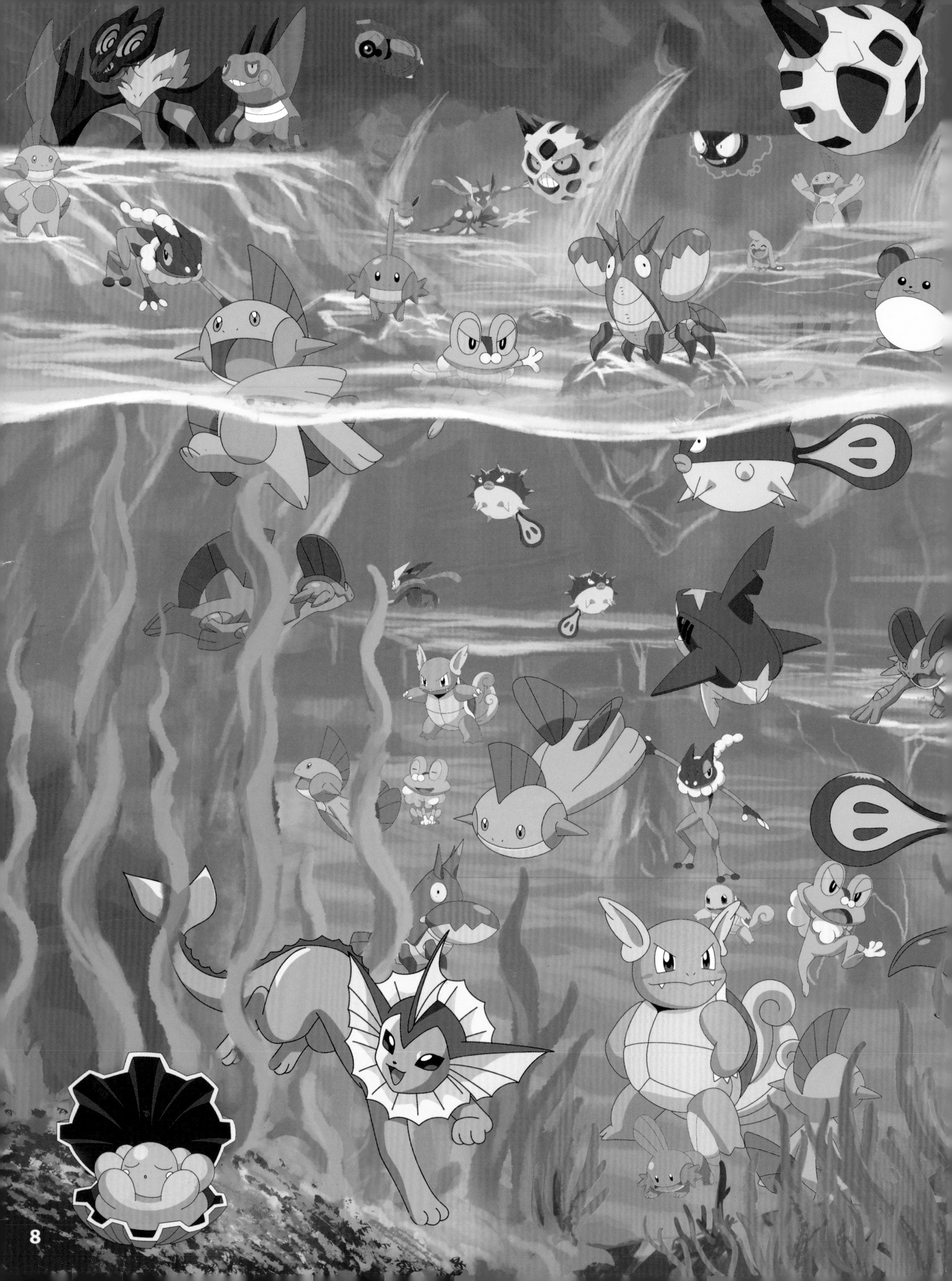

THE UNDERGROUND LAKE

Along the ice shelf, Eevee and Pikachu discover the domain of Vaporeon, a Water-type Pokémon. The Pokémon play with the seaweed and splash in the waterfalls. Have you found Pikachu and Eevee?

LOOK FOR...

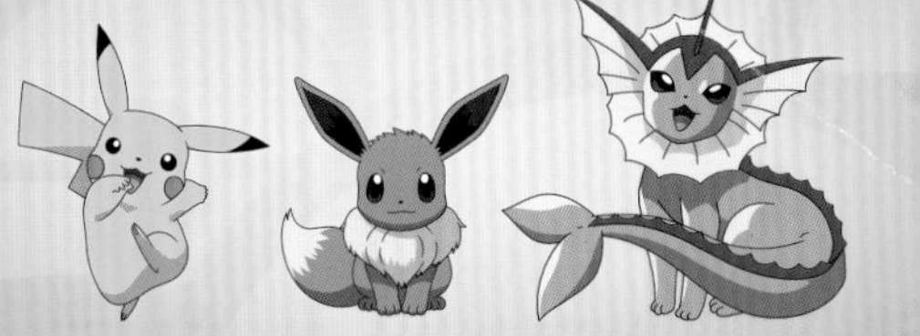

Pikachu **Eevee** **Vaporeon**

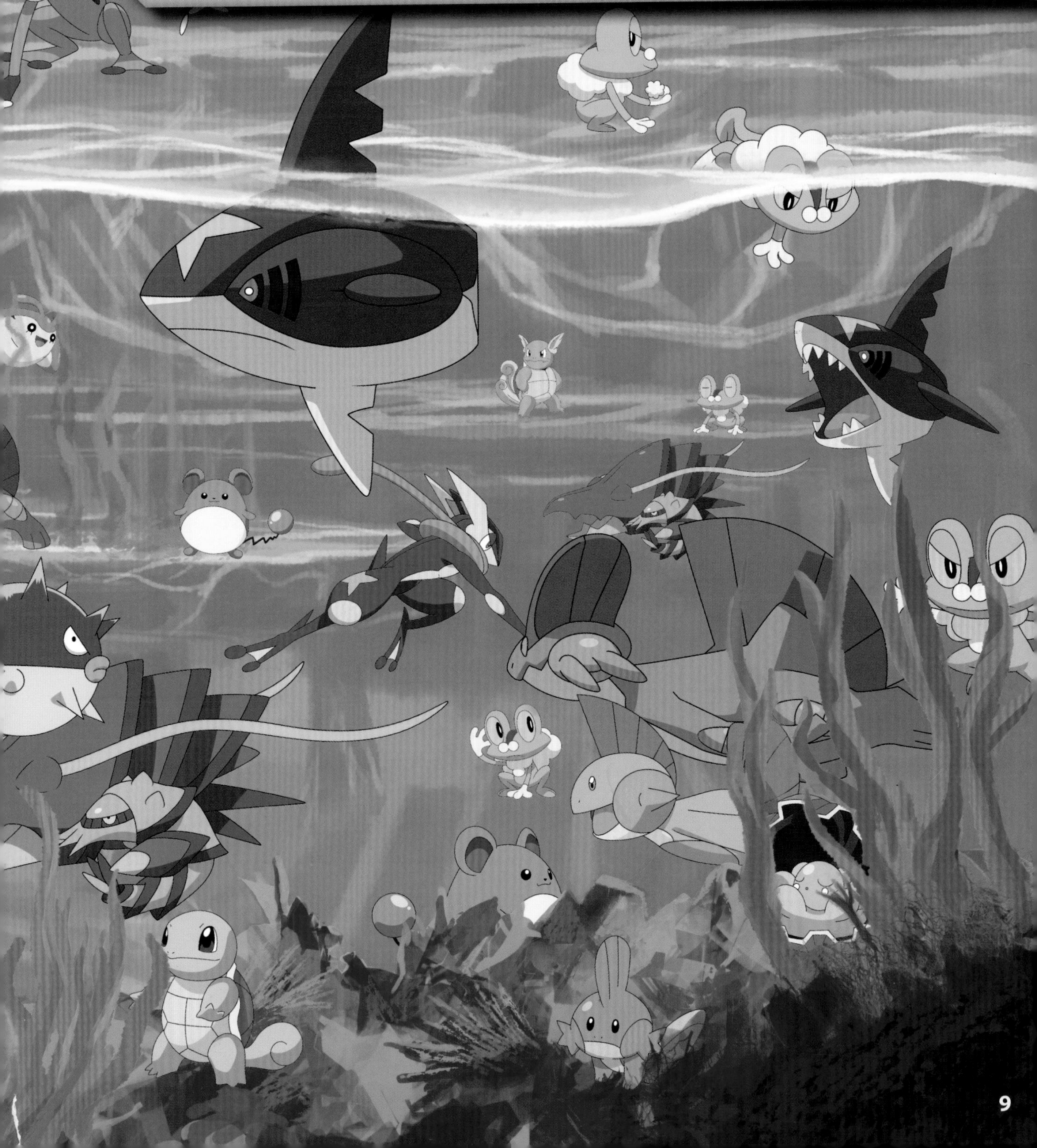

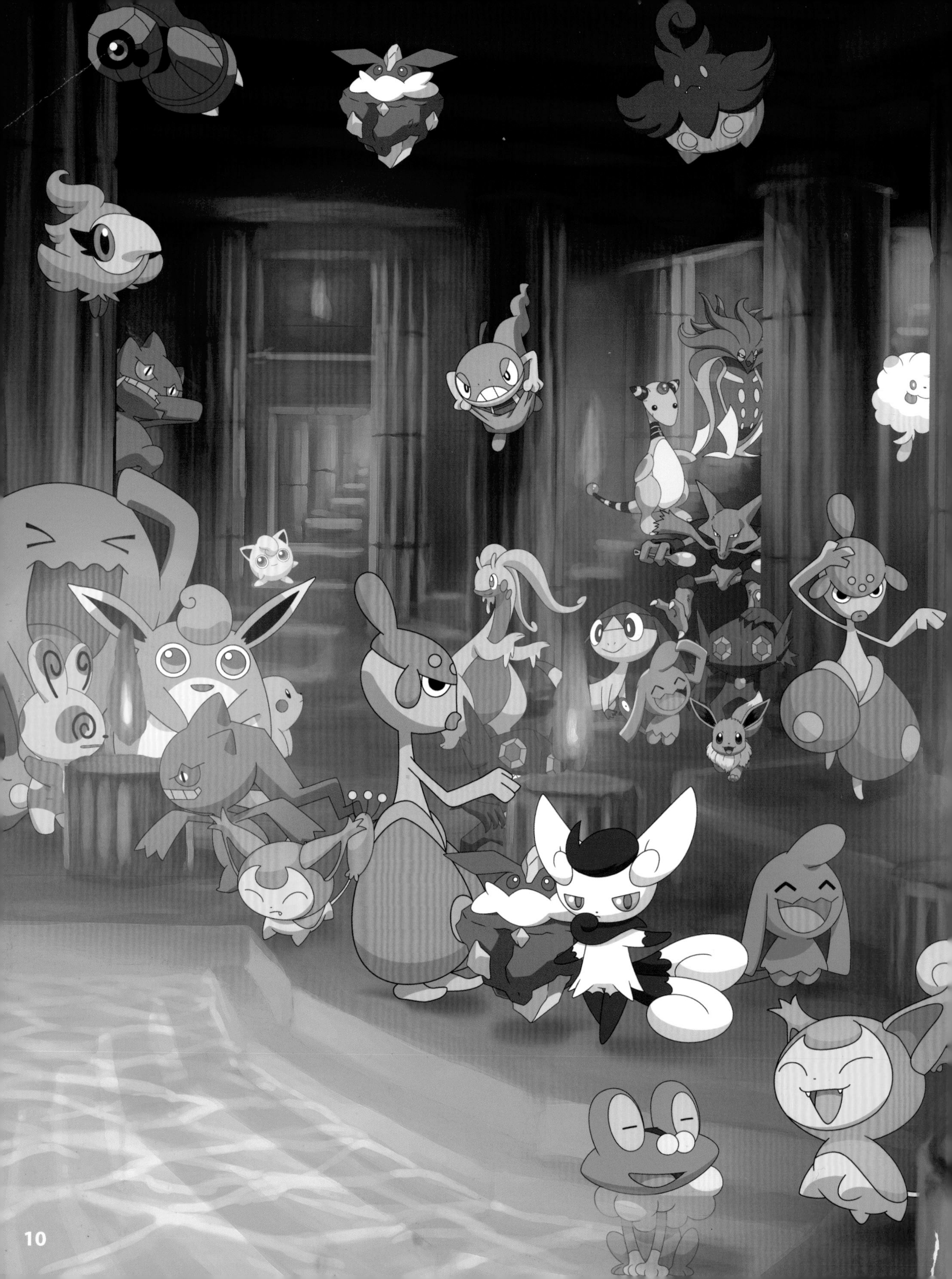

IN THE GLOW OF CANDLELIGHT

Leaving the lake, our two friends enter the palace of Psychic-type Pokémon! It's a mysterious place, but Espeon is there to reassure them and help them get to the exit. Can you see where they are right now?

LOOK FOR...

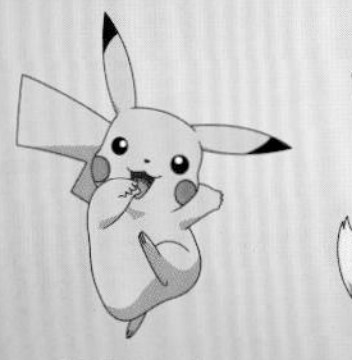

Pikachu

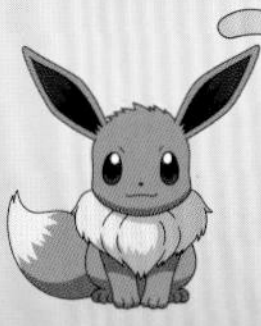

Eevee

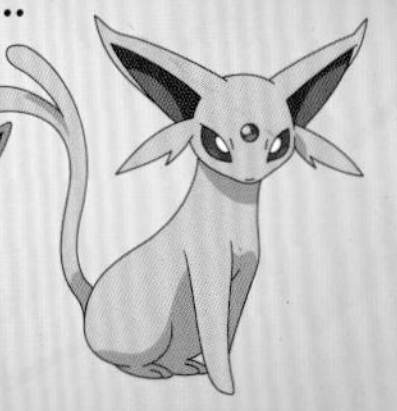

Espeon

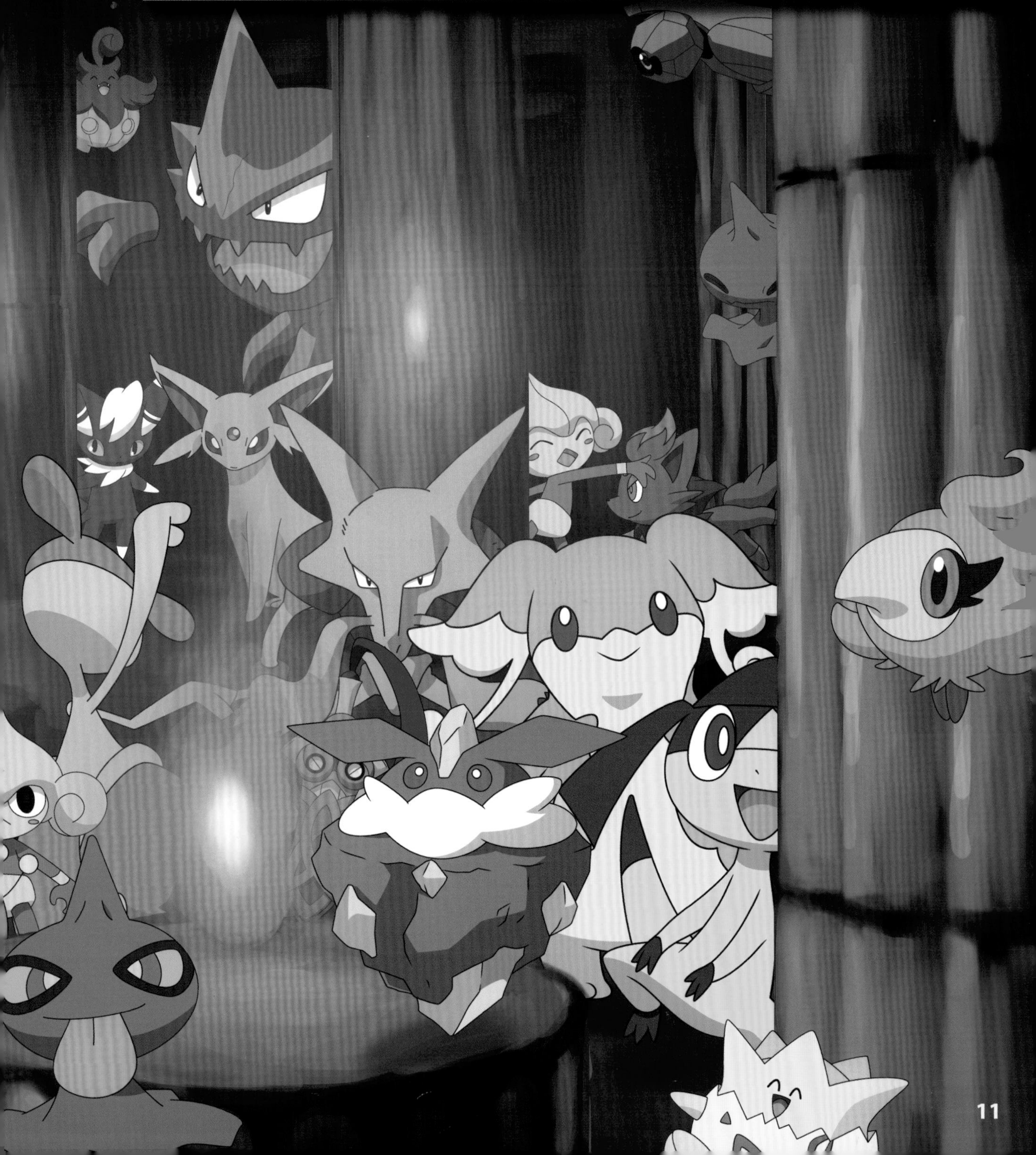

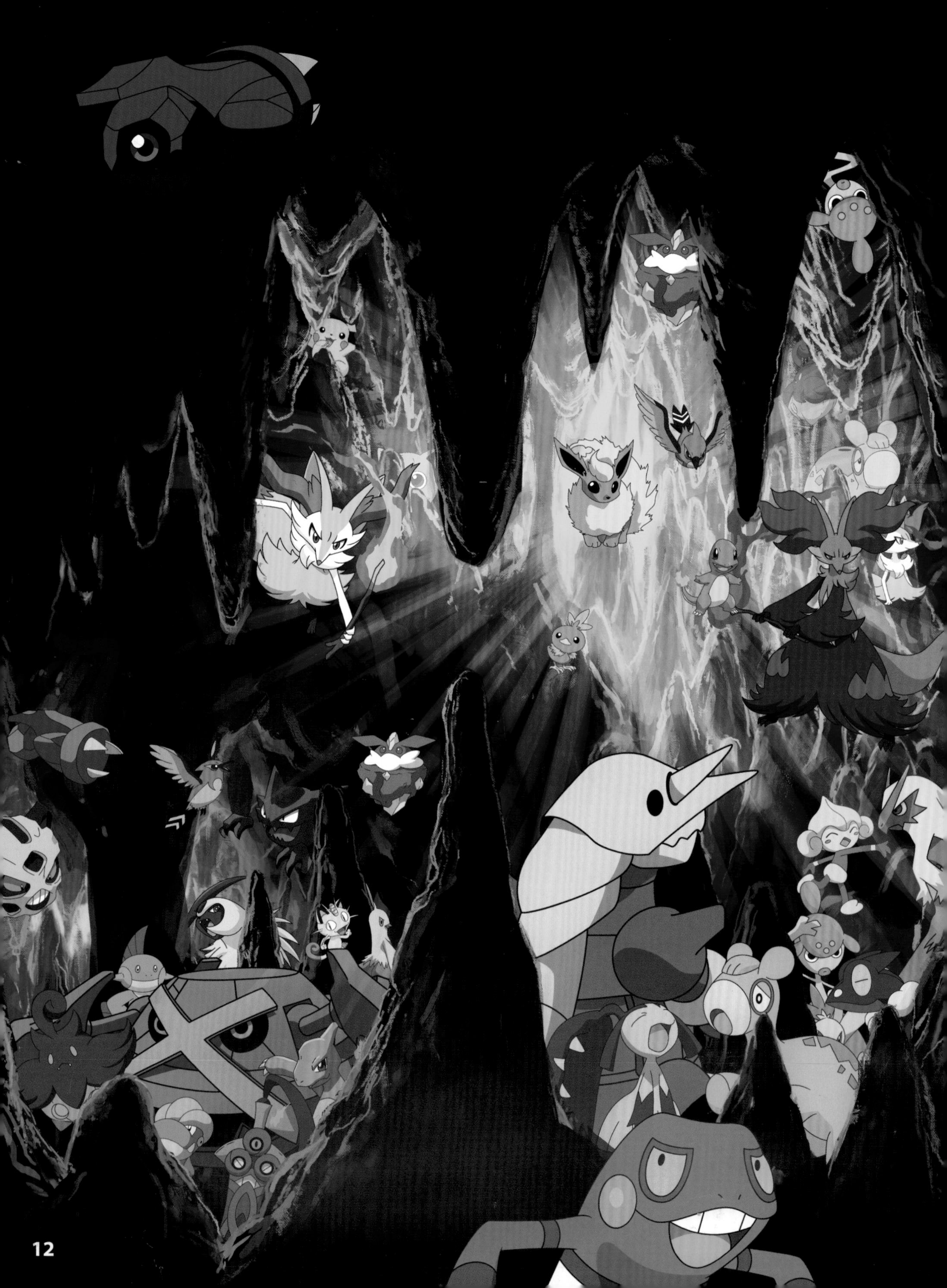

UNDERGROUND PASSAGE

Pikachu and Eevee must make their way through a dark cave, but Flareon is there to light the way with its flame. Our heroes can see all kinds of Pokémon here, and finally they spot daylight at the end of the path!

LOOK FOR...

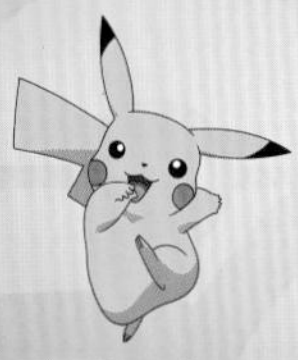

Pikachu

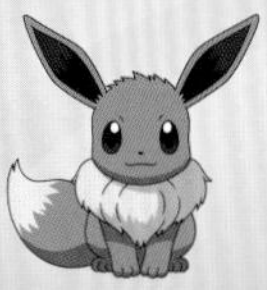

Eevee

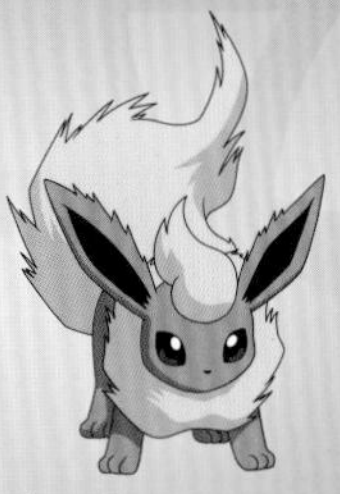

Flareon

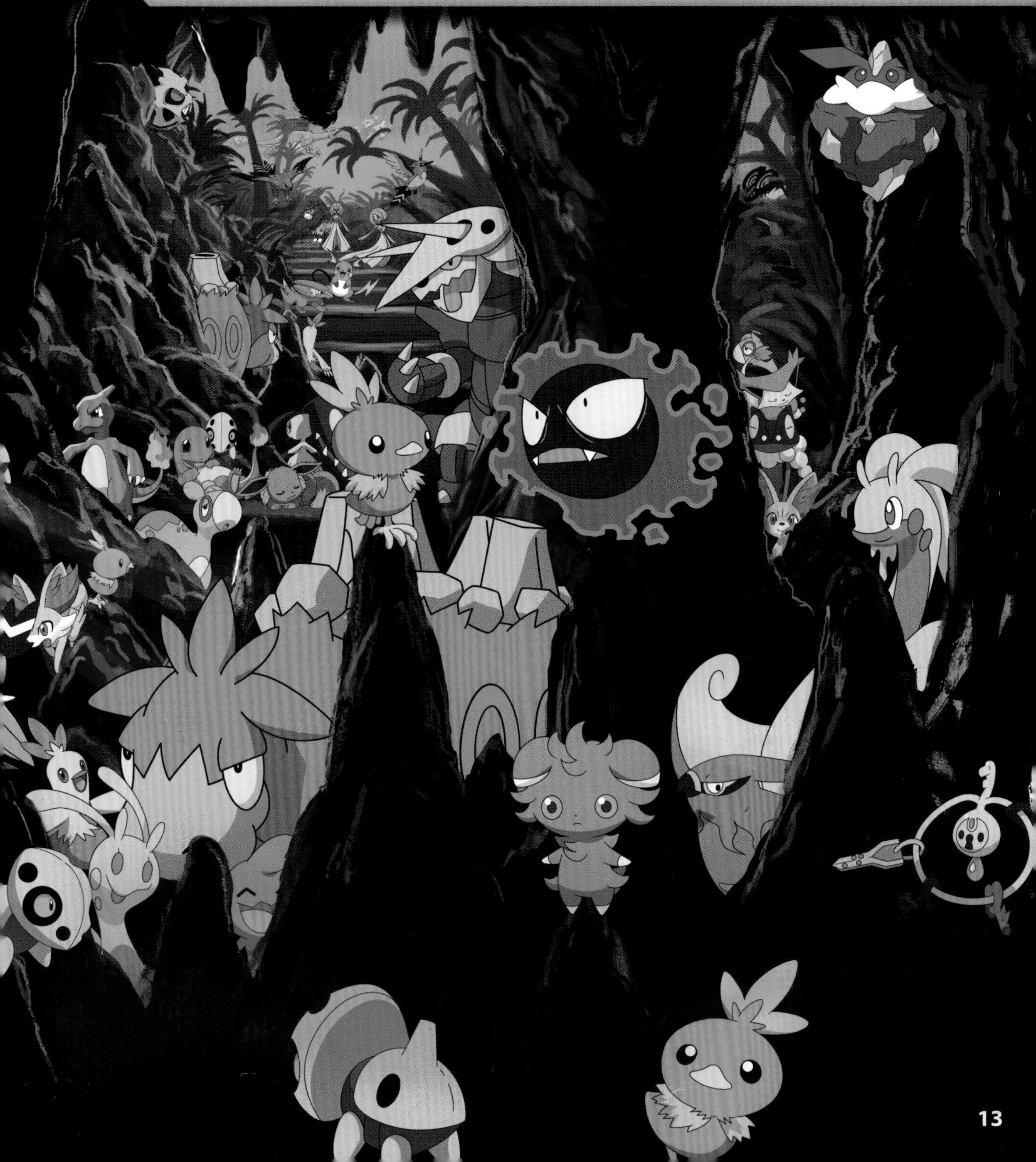

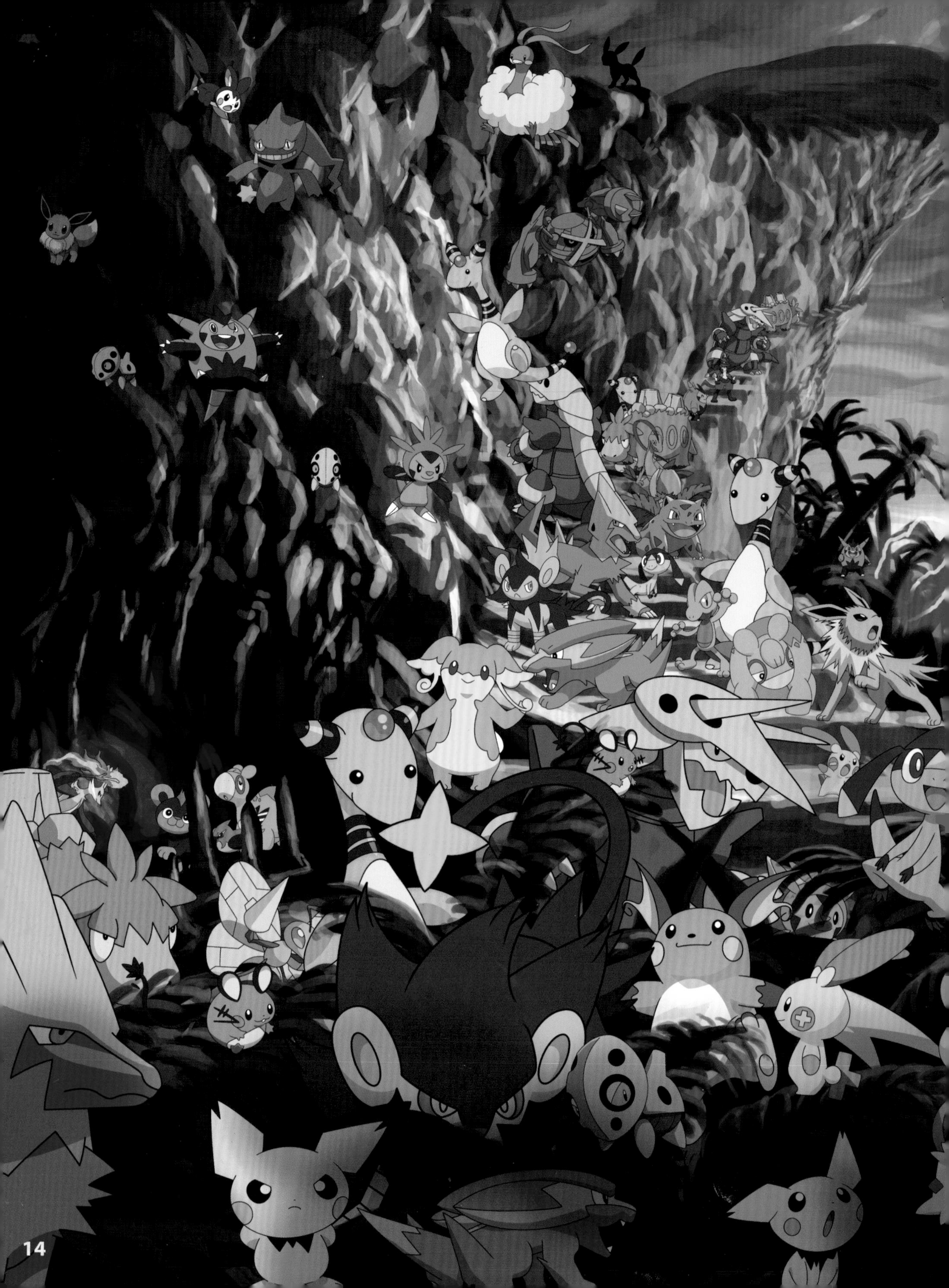

HURRICANE WARNING

Outside of the cave, there's a storm brewing! Jolteon and all the Electric-type Pokémon are having fun, while the other Pokémon look for cover! But what is that mysterious shadow on the cliff?

LOOK FOR...

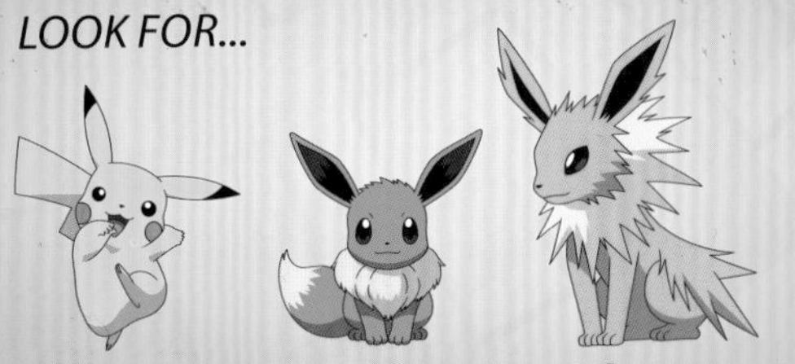

Pikachu **Eevee** **Jolteon**

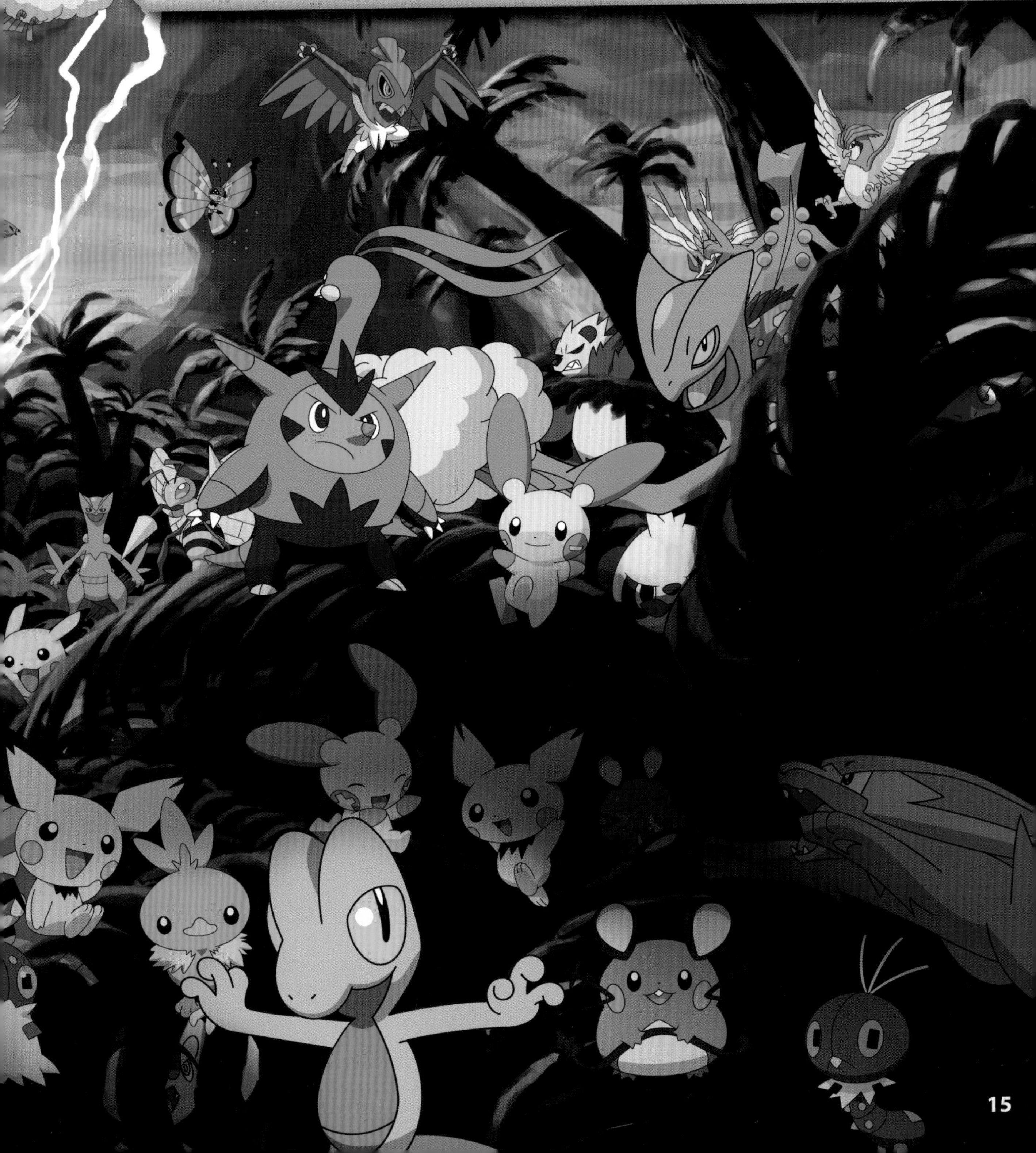

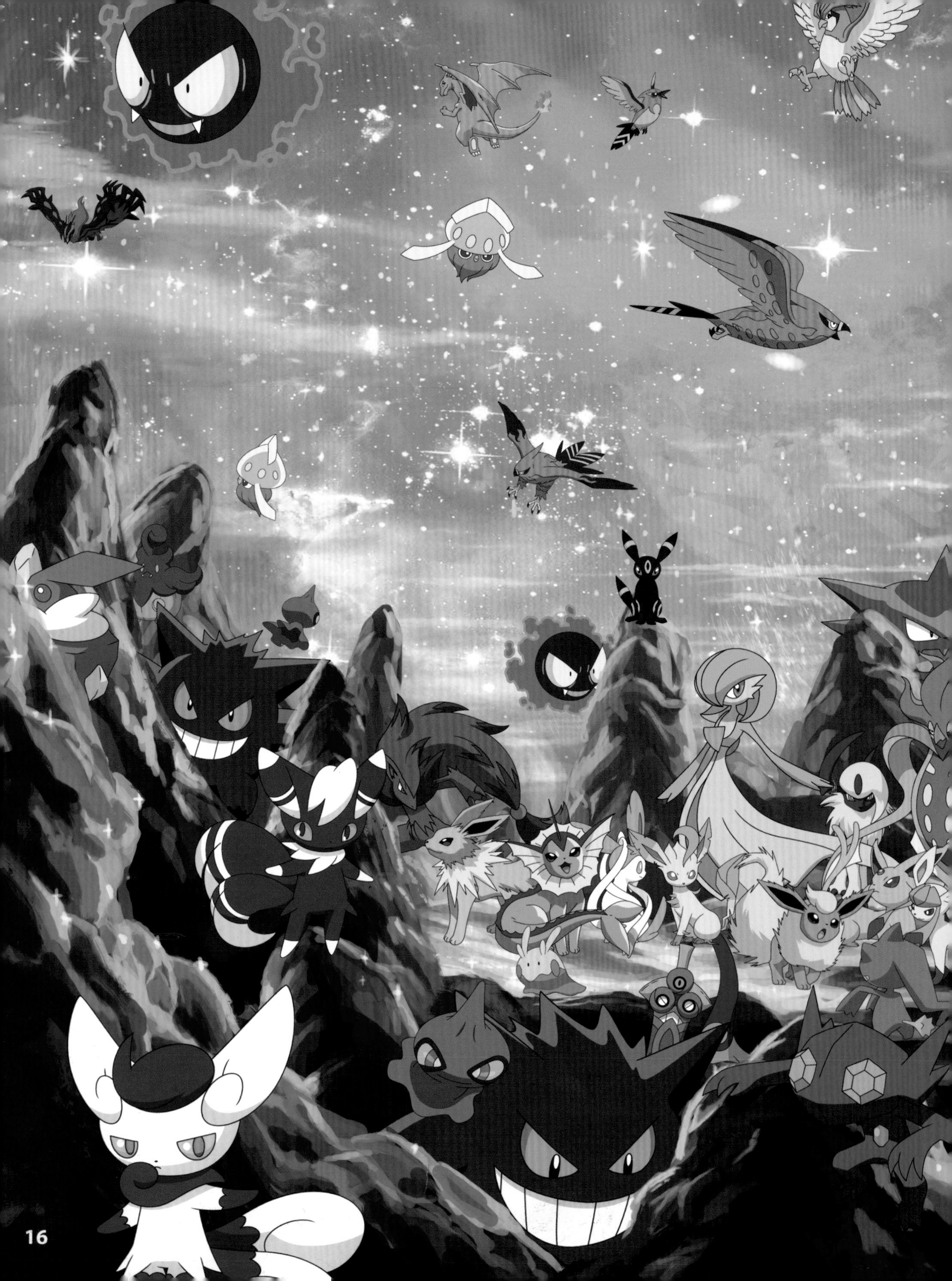

A FAIRY SPECTACLE

It's Umbreon, the Moonlight Pokémon! Umbreon and all its friends are having a party on this beautiful starry night! The Pokémon are having fun, and Pikachu thanks Eevee for this incredible trip. But…where did they go?

LOOK FOR...

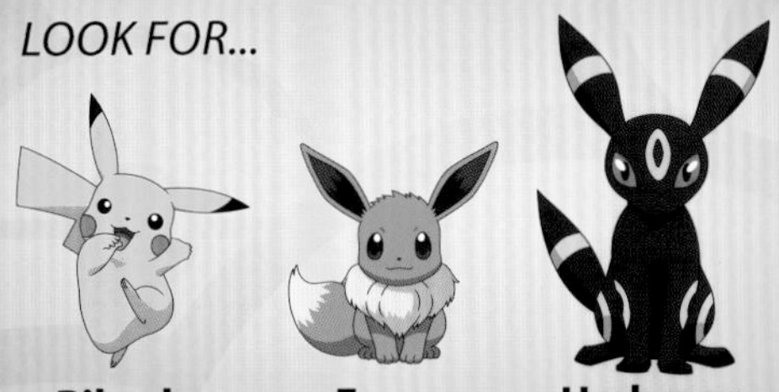

Pikachu **Eevee** **Umbreon**

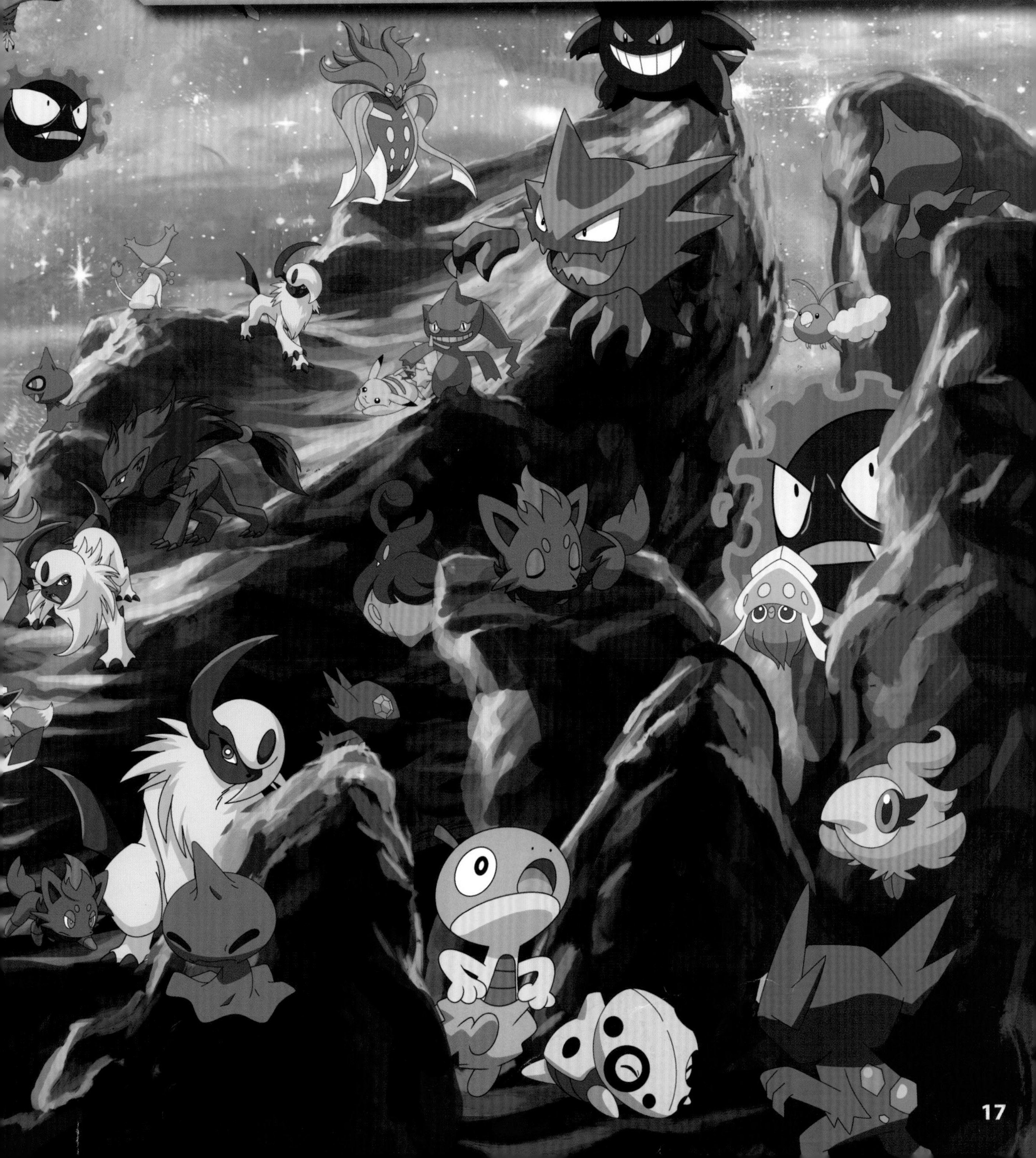

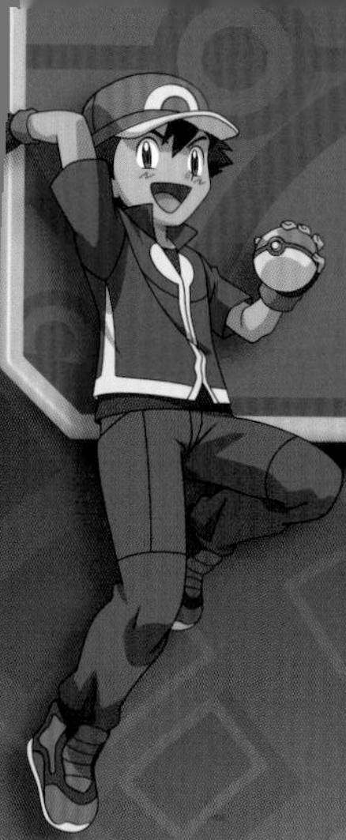

THE ULTIMATE CHALLENGE

Have you completed your mission and found all of the Pokémon in each of the scenes? If so, you're ready for the next challenge! Only the most exceptional Pokémon Trainers will succeed!

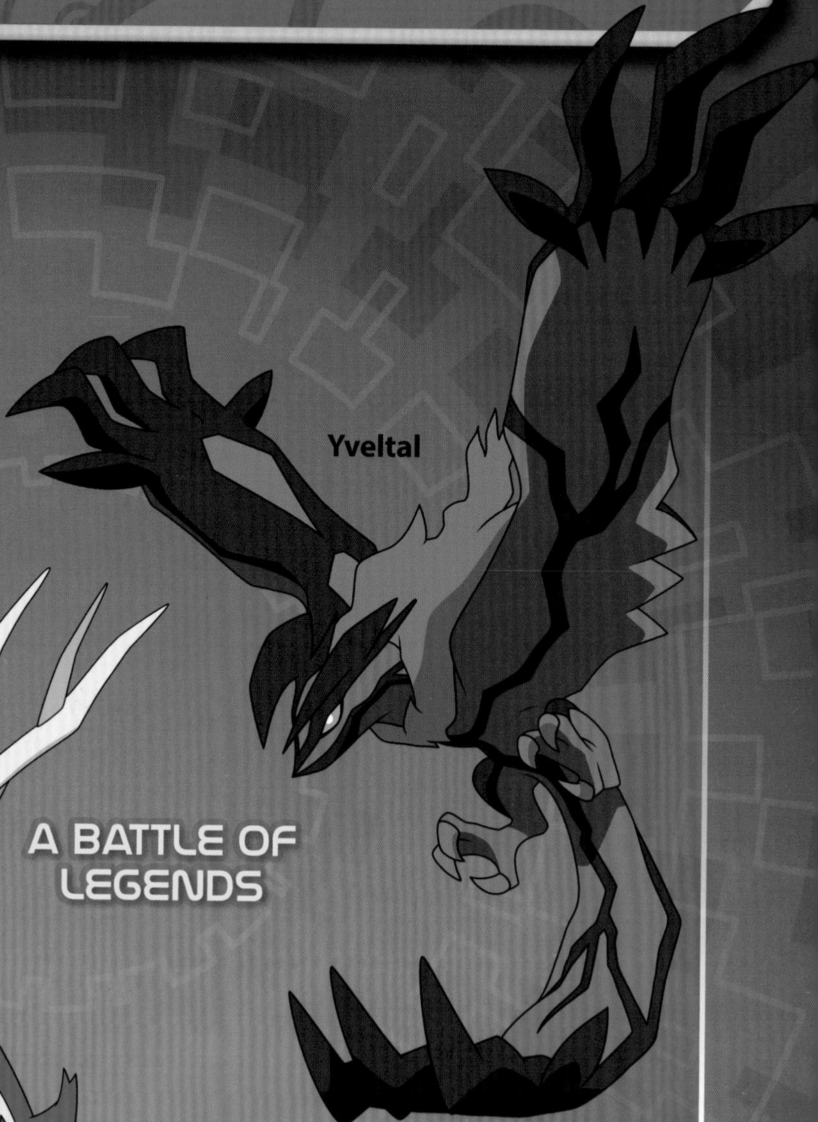

Yveltal

A BATTLE OF LEGENDS

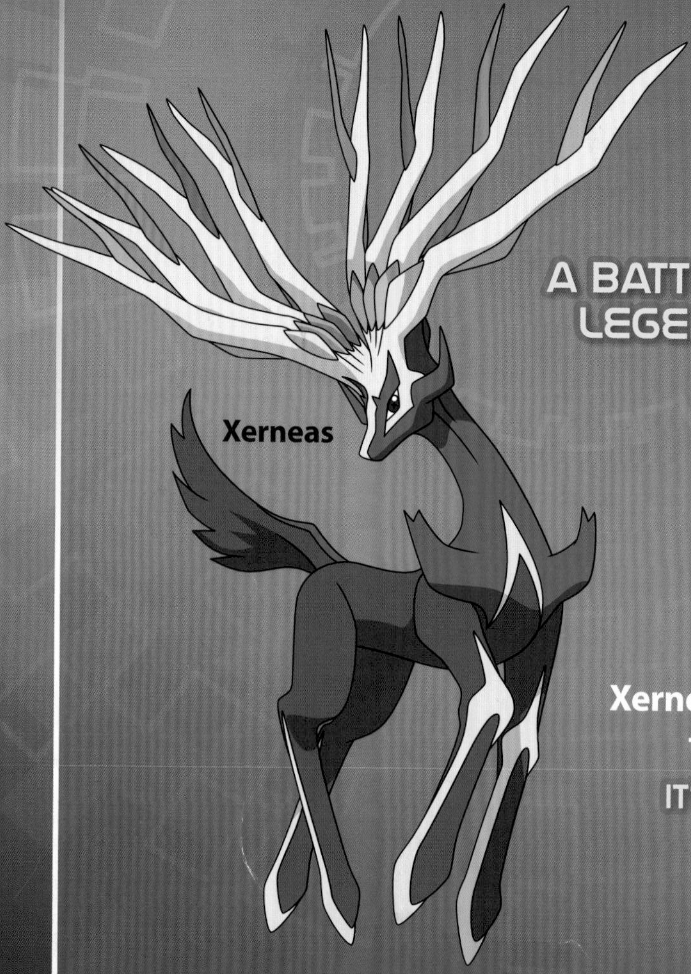

Xerneas

Xerneas and Yveltal are hiding in the pages of this story:

IT'S TIME TO FIND THEM!

POKÉMON IN THIS STORY

PIKACHU

When Pikachu senses danger, it emits a strong electric current from the pouches inside its cheeks. Its jigsaw tail can sometimes attract lightning during a storm.

Pichu → **Pikachu** → Raichu

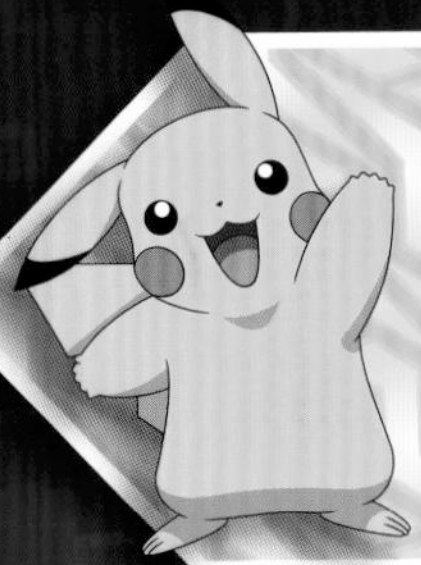

CATEGORY:
MOUSE POKÉMON

TYPE: ELECTRIC

HEIGHT: 1'04"

WEIGHT: 13.2 lbs

CATEGORY:
EVOLUTION POKÉMON

TYPE: NORMAL

HEIGHT: 1'00"

WEIGHT: 14.3 lbs

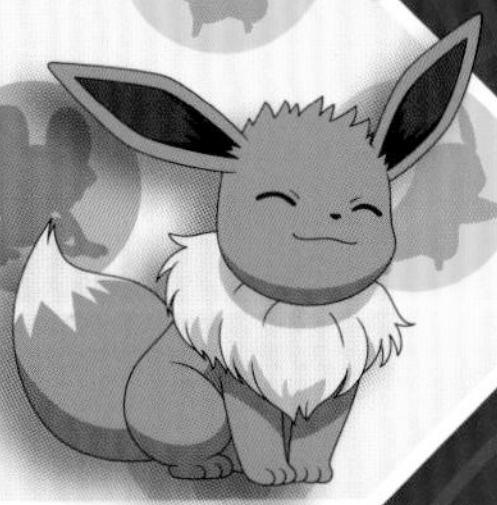

EEVEE

Its astonishing capacity for adaptation allows Eevee to evolve into different Pokémon according to its environment. This makes it possible for Eevee to withstand extreme conditions.

Eevee → Vaporeon or Jolteon or Flareon or Espeon or Umbreon or Leafeon or Glaceon or Sylveon

THE 8 EVOLUTIONS OF EEVEE:

VAPOREON

Vaporeon's cellular structure resembles that of a water molecule, which is why it can dissipate and disappear in aquatic environments. It loves a beautiful beach.

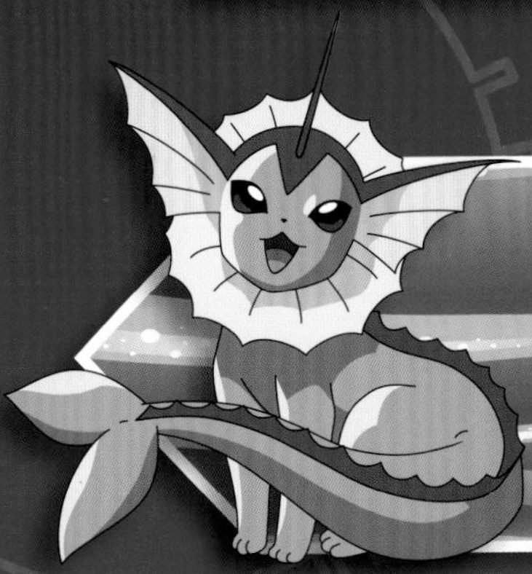

CATEGORY:
BUBBLE JET POKÉMON

TYPE: WATER

HEIGHT: 3'03"

WEIGHT: 63.9 lbs

CATEGORY:
LIGHTNING POKÉMON

TYPE: ELECTRIC

HEIGHT: 2'07"

WEIGHT: 54.0 lbs

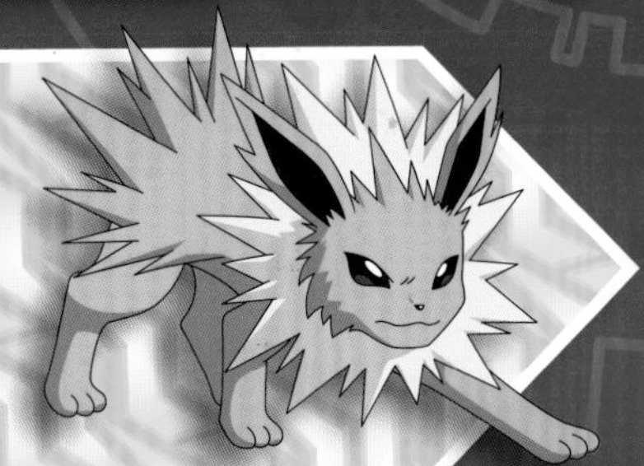

JOLTEON

When its fur spikes up all of a sudden, it means Jolteon is charged with electricity. It collects the electricity from the surrounding air and uses it for its high-voltage attacks.

FLAREON

The pouch of fire inside Flareon's body feeds its flaming breath. While it prepares to fight, its body temperature can go up to 1,650°F.

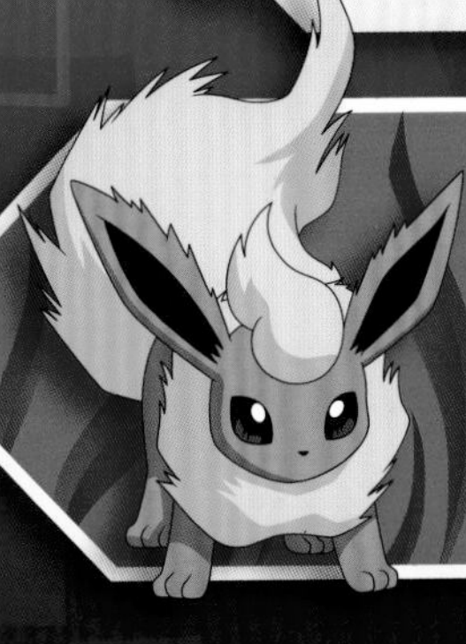

CATEGORY:
FLAME POKÉMON

TYPE: FIRE

HEIGHT: 2'11"

WEIGHT: 55.1 lbs

ESPEON

Espeon's incredibly sensitive fur means it can detect the slightest movement in the air. This allows Espeon to feel changes in temperature and to predict its opponent's movements.

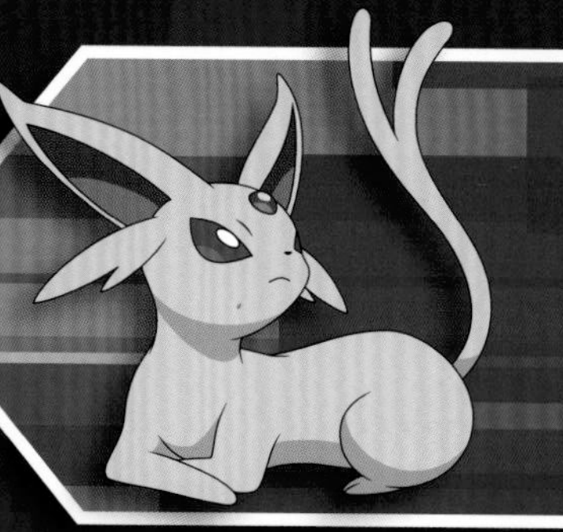

CATEGORY: SUN POKÉMON

TYPE: PSYCHIC

HEIGHT: 2'11"

WEIGHT: 58.4 lbs

CATEGORY: MOONLIGHT POKÉMON

TYPE: DARK

HEIGHT: 3'03"

WEIGHT: 59.5 lbs

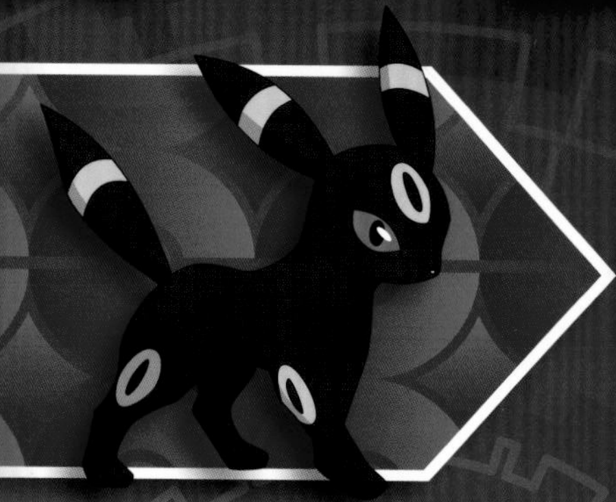

UMBREON

Umbreon's genetic structure is influenced by moonlight. When there's a full moon, the rings on its body emit a faint glow.

LEAFEON

When Leafeon absorbs sunlight to photosynthesize, it releases fresh, pure air. It frequently naps under the sun to re-energize.

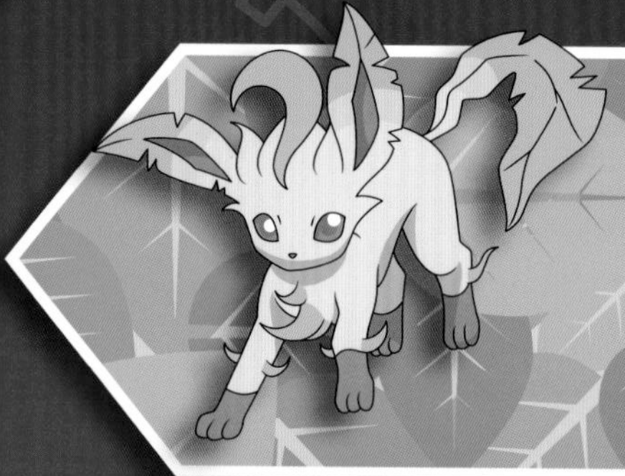

CATEGORY: VERDANT POKÉMON

TYPE: GRASS

HEIGHT: 3'03"

WEIGHT: 56.2 lbs

CATEGORY: FRESH SNOW POKÉMON

TYPE: ICE

HEIGHT: 2'07"

WEIGHT: 57.1 lbs

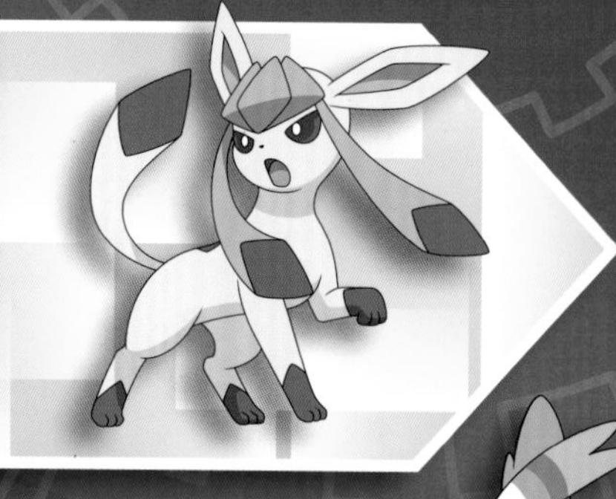

GLACEON

Glaceon has incredible control over its body temperature. It can freeze its own fur and pluck frozen hairs, which become dangerous needles against its adversaries.

SYLVEON

To keep others from fighting, Sylveon projects a calming aura from its feelers, which look like flowing ribbons. It wraps those ribbons around its Trainer's arm when they walk together.

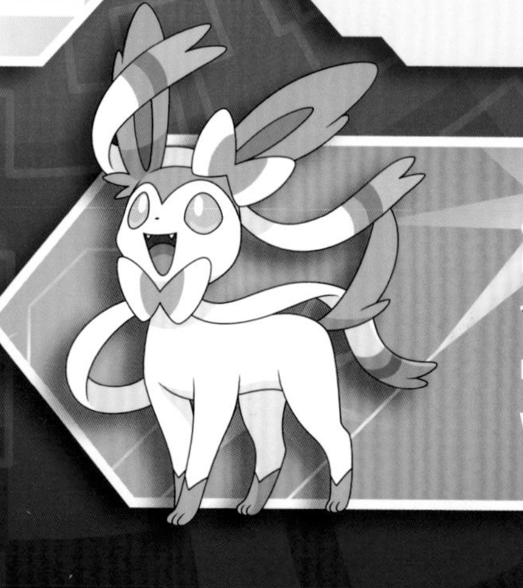

CATEGORY: INTERTWINING POKÉMON

TYPE: FAIRY

HEIGHT: 3'03"

WEIGHT: 51.8 lbs

⊙ POKÉMON QUIZ

How well do you know your Pokémon? Are you ready to become a super Trainer? Answer these questions to find out!

① **Seek and find at least 3 Water-type Pokémon on pages 4 and 5.**

....

② **Are these Water-type Pokémon?**

☐ Yes ☐ No

③ **Is Sceptile at least 6 feet tall?**

☐ Yes ☐ No

④ **Which of these Pokémon evolves from Froakie?** ☐ Croagunk ☐ Frogadier

Hint: Find this Pokémon on pages 8 and 9.

⑤ **Which one of these is NOT an Ice-type Pokémon?**

☐ Glaceon    ☐ Snorunt    ☐ Wobbuffet

⑥ **Arrange the following Pokémon in the order of their Evolution:**

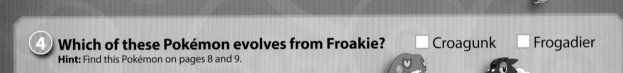

☐ Mega Garchomp   ☐ Gabite    ☐ Gible    ☐ Garchomp

Answers: 1. For example, Froakie, Frogadier, Greninja, Squirtle, etc. **2.** No. Croagunk is a Poison- and Fighting-type Pokémon. **3.** No. It is 5'07". **4.** Frogadier. **5.** Wobbuffet. **6.** Gible, Gabite, Garchomp, Mega Garchomp.

21

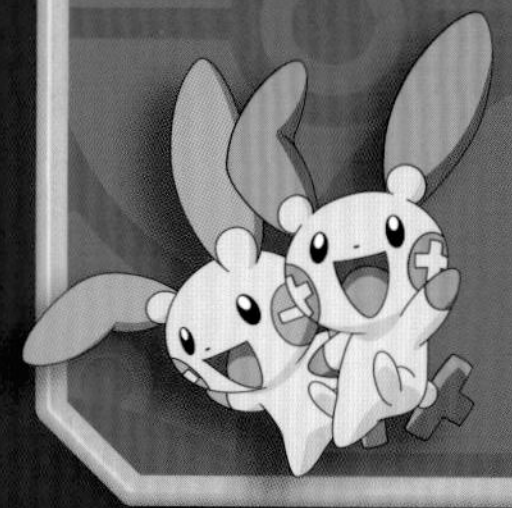

EXPLORE THE WORLD OF POKÉMON

Pokémon live in unique regions…but their scenes have gotten all mixed up! One of these strips does not appear in this book. Can you find it?

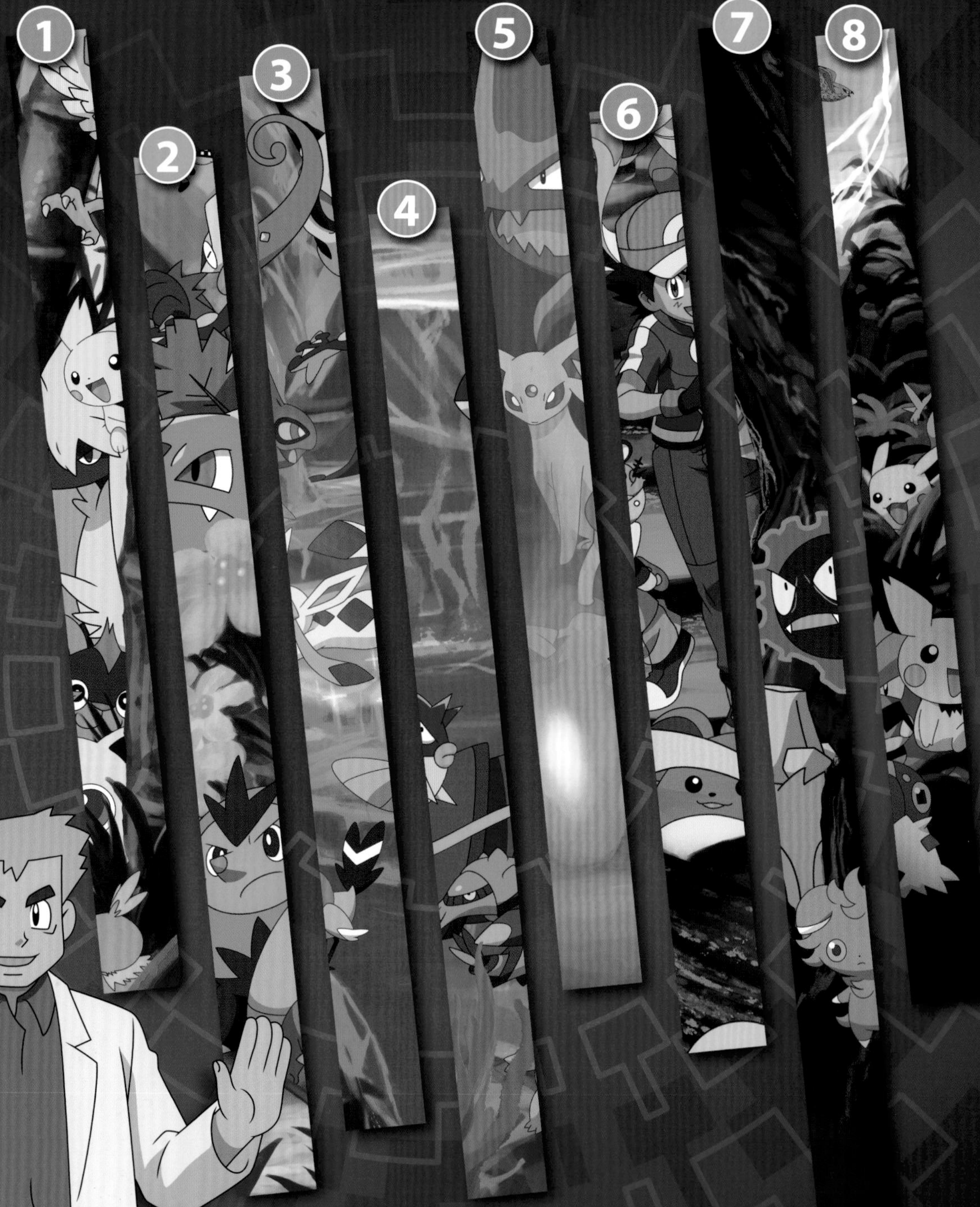
1
2
3
4
5
6
7
8

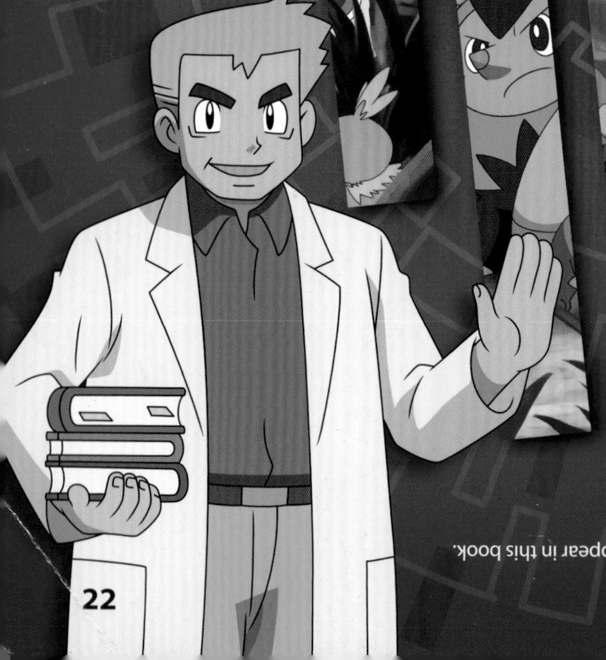

Answer: Strip number 6 does not appear in this book.

PIKACHU AND FRIENDS

Pikachu and Eevee meet in the forest!

QUESTION 1: But where's Pikachu? Find it!

QUESTION 2: Pikachu is what type of Pokémon?
- ☐ Fire-type
- ☐ Electric-type
- ☐ Dark-type

QUESTION 3: What is the Evolution of Pikachu?

QUESTION 4: Pikachu can shoot lightning from its tail. True or false?

QUESTION 5: Does Pikachu have the same number of toes on its front paws as it does on its rear paws?

Look very carefully at this picture for two minutes and then turn the page...

Answers: 1. It's at the top in the back left behind Pichu. **2.** Electric-type. **3.** Raichu. **4.** True. **5.** No, it has five toes on its front paws and three on its rear paws.

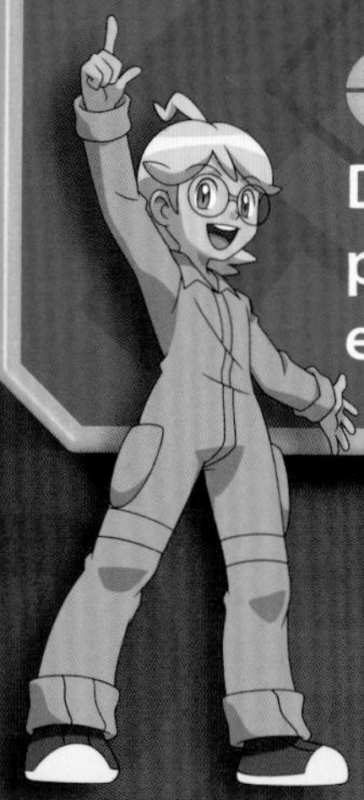

OBSERVATION SKILLS

Did you get a good look at the scene on the previous page? Are you sure? Let's find out! Check true or false for each statement without turning the page back.

	TRUE	FALSE
Ash is in the scene.		
The Pokémon are in water.		
There are two Pichu in the image.		
Pikachu is lying down.		
Ivysaur is in the scene.		
Chespin is smiling.		
There are more than ten Pokémon.		

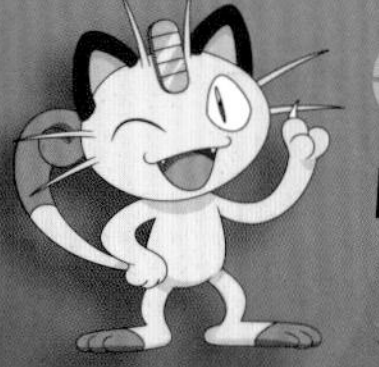

WHO AM I?

Match each Pokémon to its unique characteristic.

CLUE 1
This Pokémon illuminates points on its body to dazzle its enemies.

CLUE 2
This Pokémon can get you through any door…

CLUE 3
This Pokémon tries to intimidate opponents, but it's too cute!

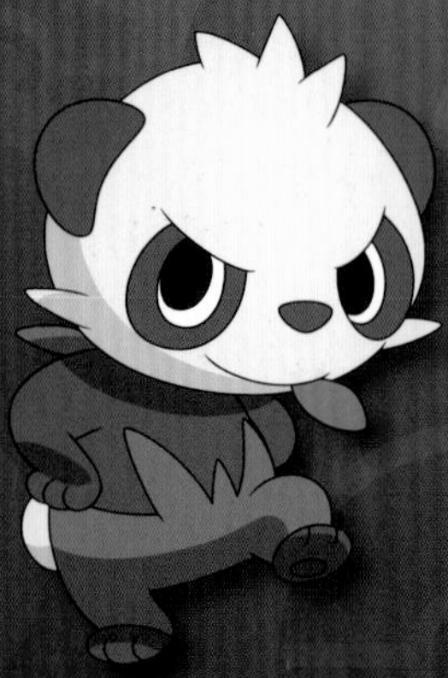

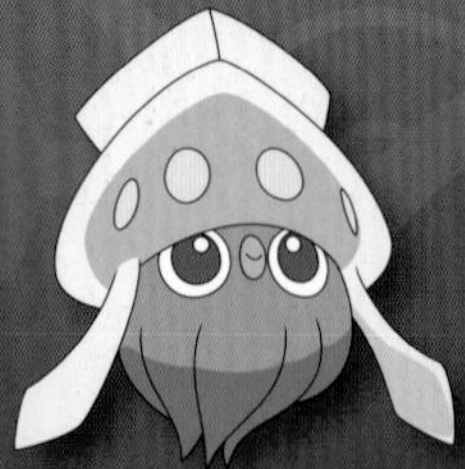

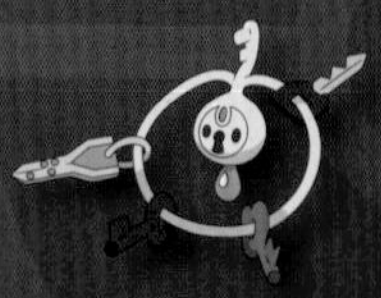

Answers: False, False (they're in the forest), True, False, False (it's Bulbasaur), True, True.
Clue 1: Inkay **Clue 2:** Klefki **Clue 3:** Pancham

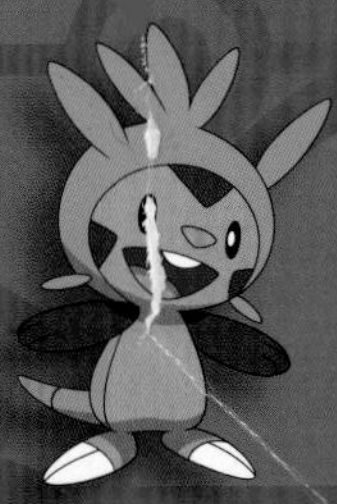

FROM SHORTEST TO TALLEST

Pikachu is 1'04" tall. Sort these Pokémon from shortest to tallest. Which Pokémon are shorter than Pikachu?

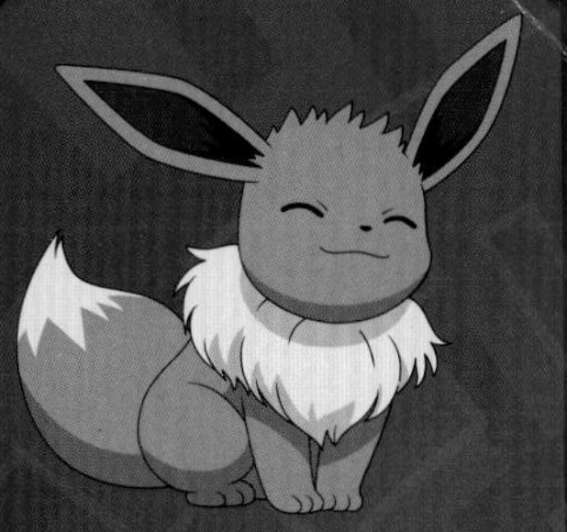

Eevee

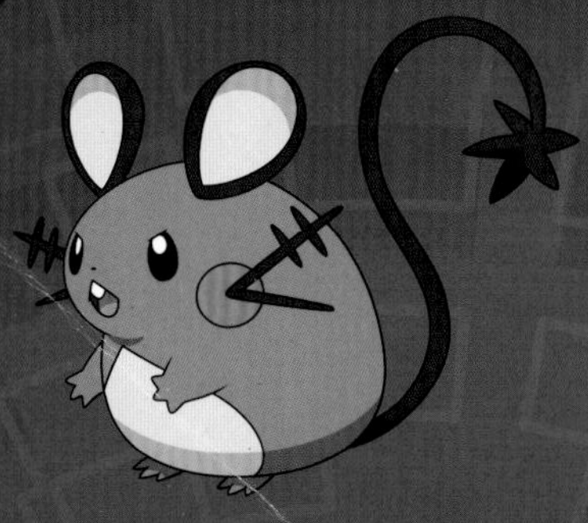

Dedenne

Pokémon	Height
Pikachu	1'04"
Eevee	1'00"
Vaporeon	3'03"
Rayquaza	23'00"
Flareon	2'11"
Sylveon	3'03"
Dedenne	0'08"

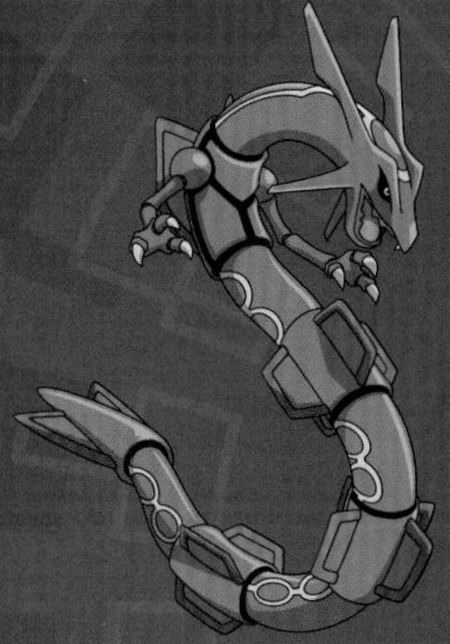

Rayquaza

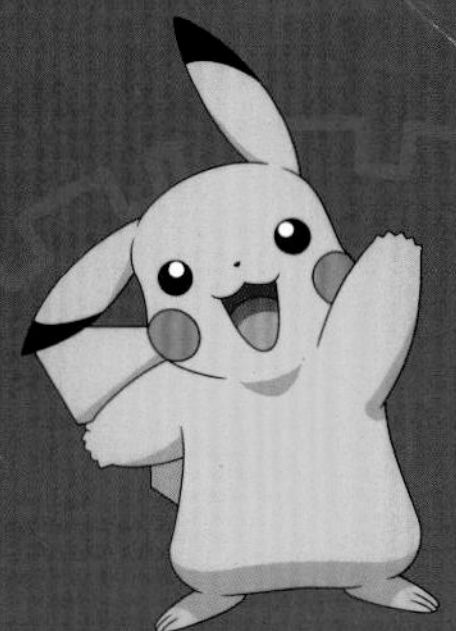

Pikachu

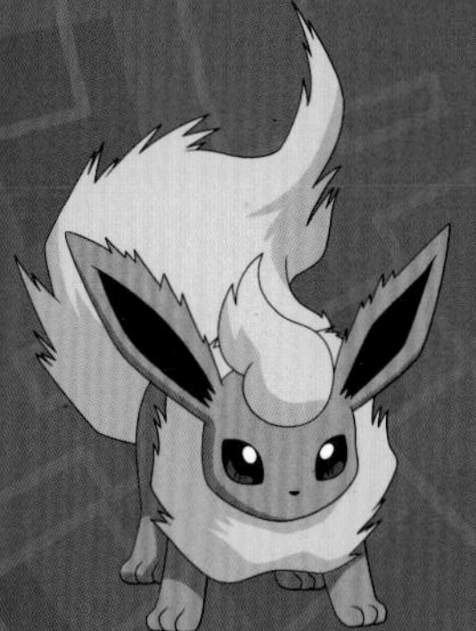

Flareon

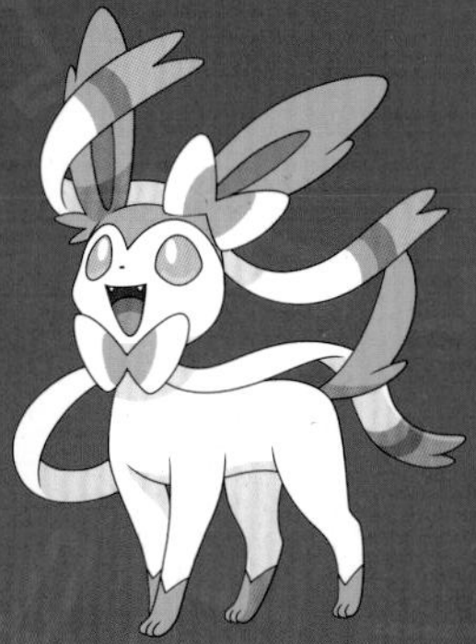

Sylveon

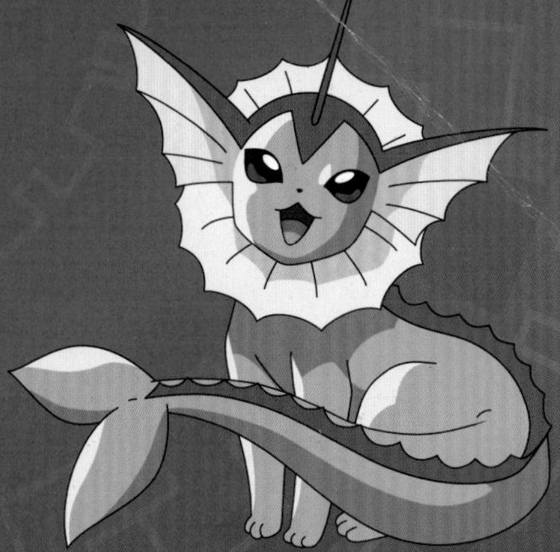

Vaporeon

–

+

Answer: Dedenne, Eevee, Pikachu, Flareon, Vaporeon and Sylveon (the same height), Rayquaza.
The Pokémon shorter than Pikachu are Dedenne and Eevee.

ALONE IN THE WORLD

One of these Pokémon doesn't have a match. Which one is it?

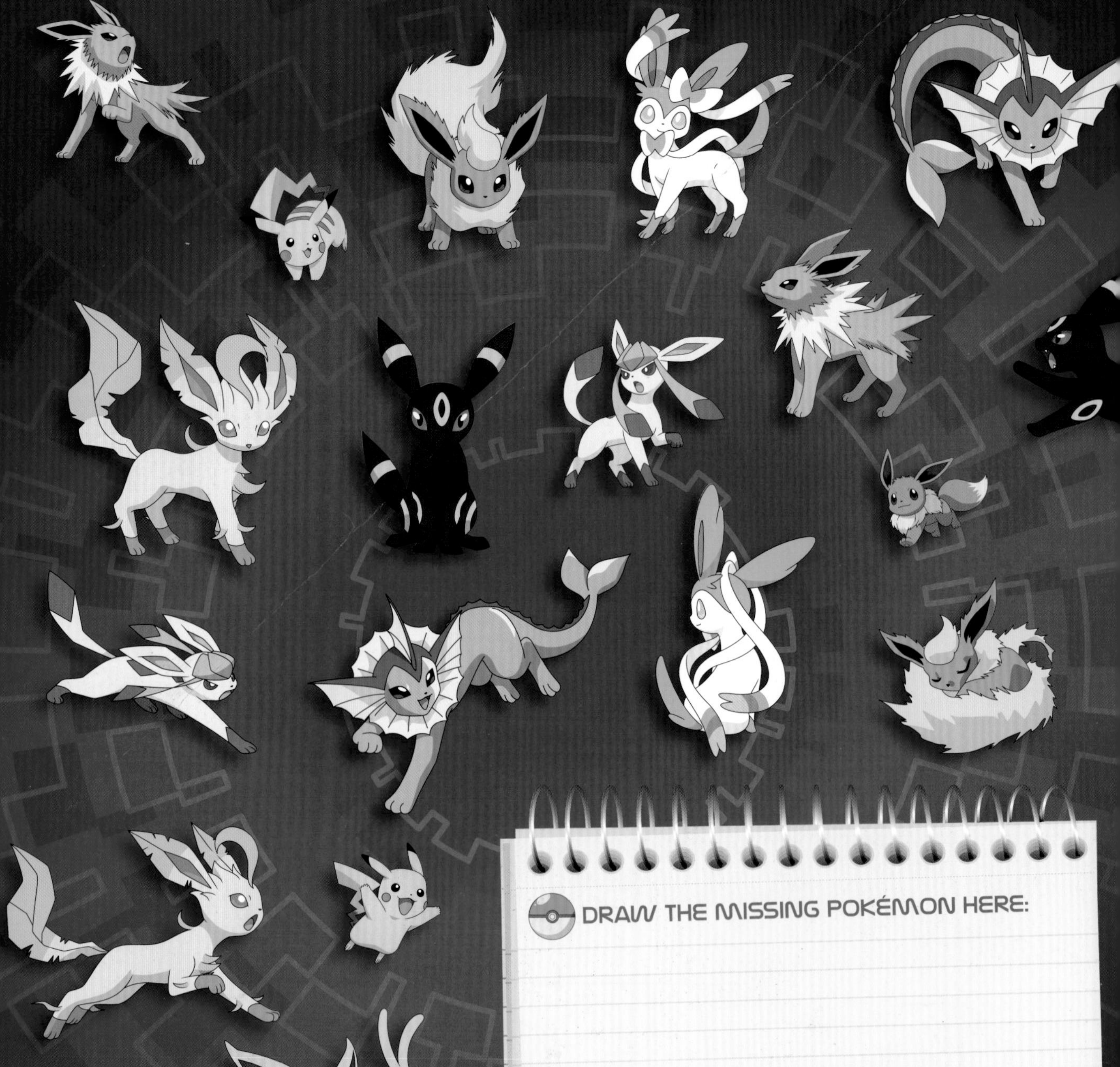

DRAW THE MISSING POKÉMON HERE:

Answer: The Pokémon that only appears once is Espeon.

NOCTURNAL VISION

Find the ten differences between these two images.

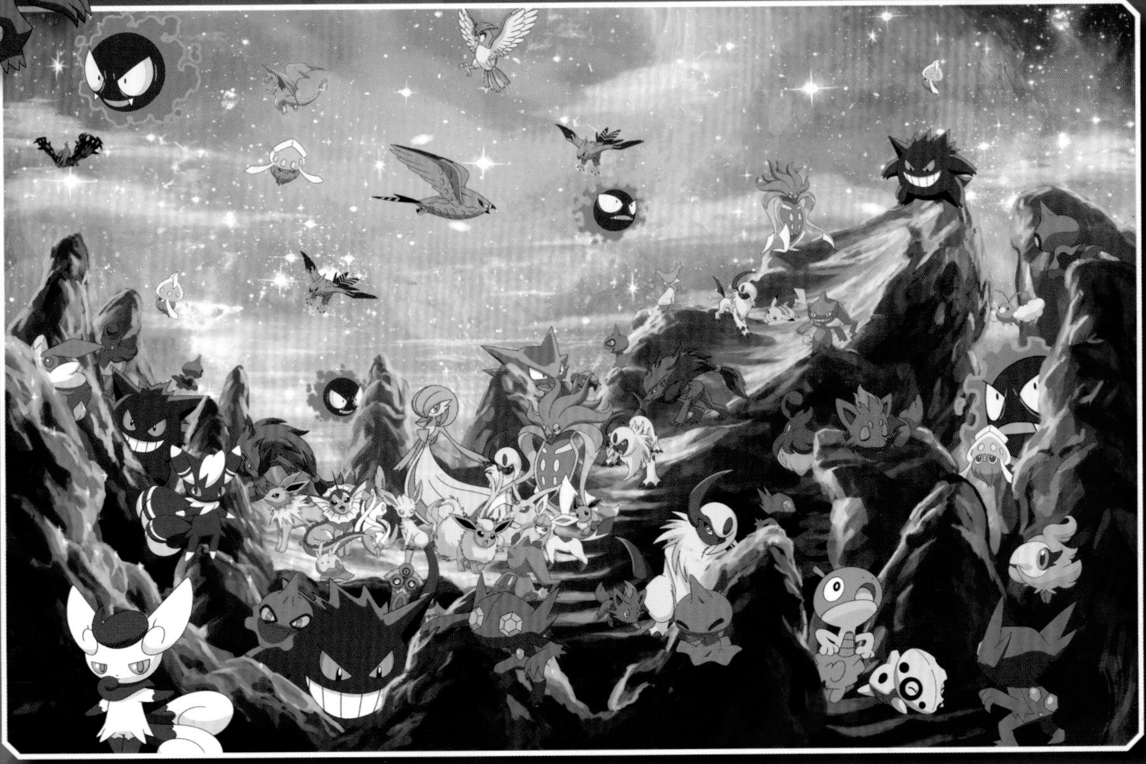

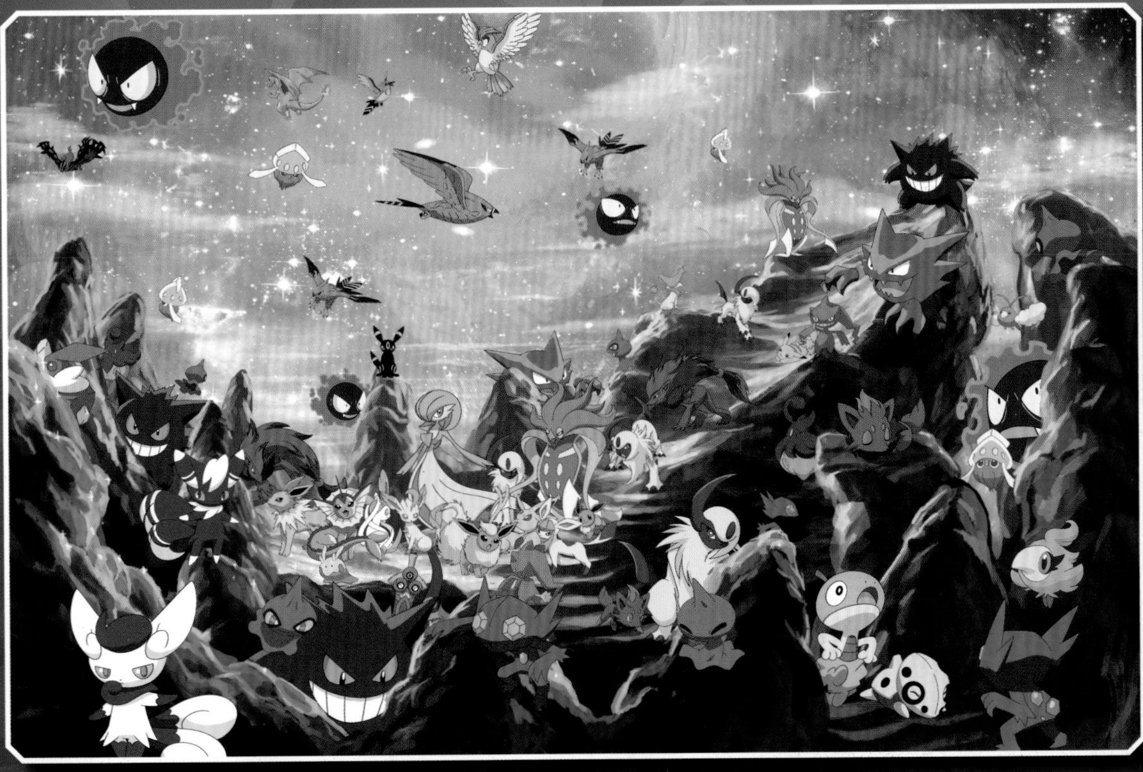

Solution on page 29.

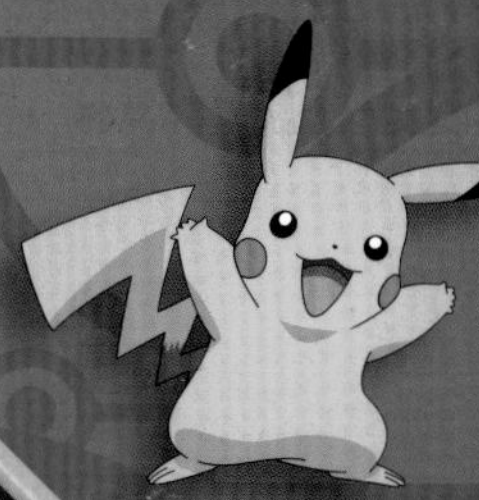

HIDE-AND-SEEK

Pikachu and friends have reunited, but there are still some challenges remaining. If you look hard, can you find the answers?

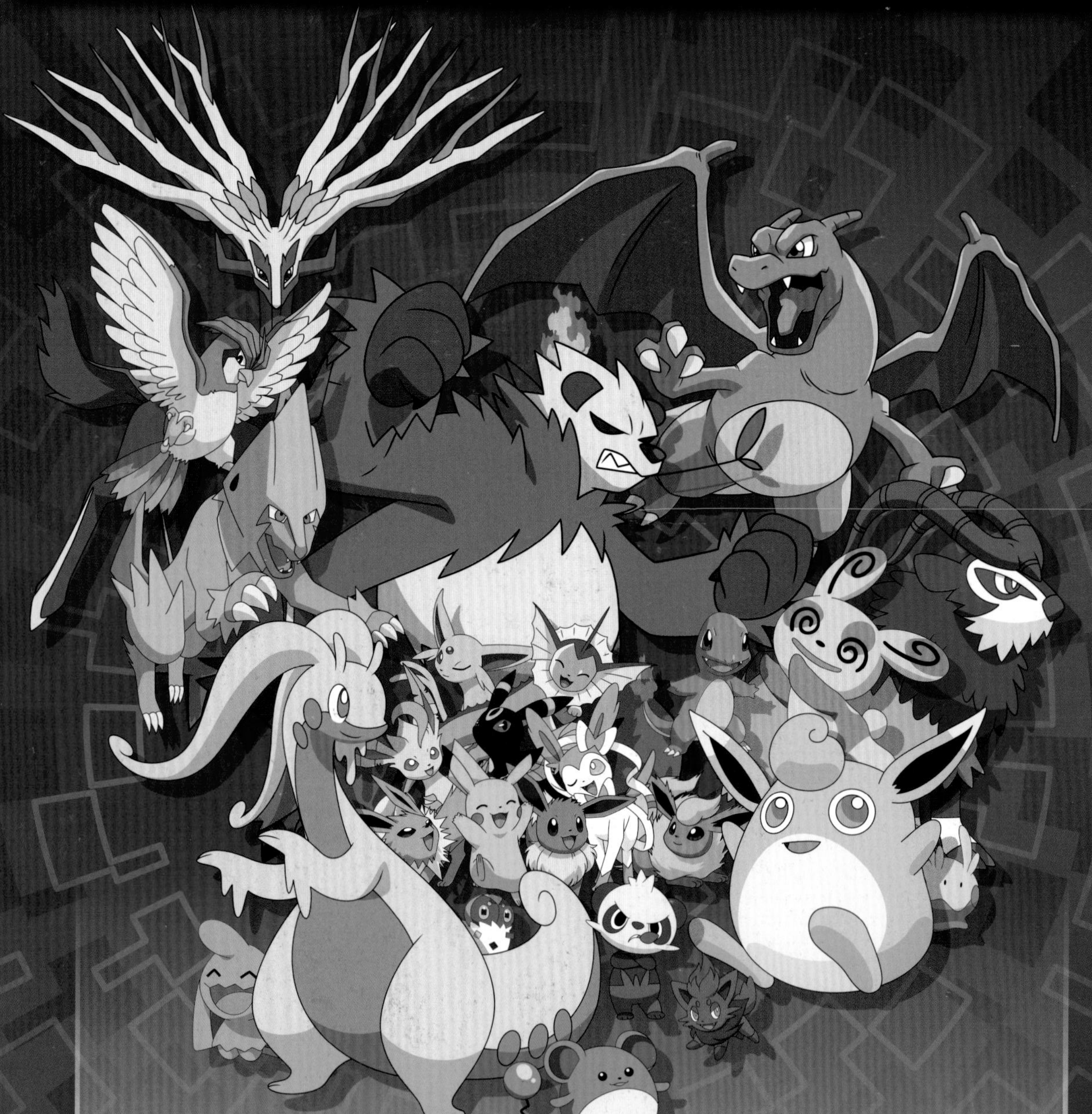

CHALLENGE 1: For starters, find Xerneas.

CHALLENGE 2: Find the Evolution of Jigglypuff.

CHALLENGE 3: One of Eevee's Evolutions is missing. Which one?

CHALLENGE 4: Which of Eevee's Evolutions regenerates in the sun?

Solution on page 29.